Lucky Four

ANNE COLVER

Lucky Four

Illustrations by ALBERT ORBAAN

DUELL, SLOAN AND PEARCE   NEW YORK

First edition

Passages from the original *Hoofprint* are reproduced by generous
permission of Ellen Pearce, editor and chief writer of that "irregular, irresistible chronicle."

Library of Congress Catalogue Card Number: 60-12843

MANUFACTURED IN THE UNITED STATES OF AMERICA

VAN REES PRESS • NEW YORK

To

PATSY EDWARDS AND SUE STUMP

WHO INTRODUCED ME TO

the *Merrymakers* of Kansas

and to

THE GHOST OF THE REAL CUDDLES

WHO PERISHED IN THE LINE OF 4-H DUTY

THIS BOOK IS DEDICATED

NOTE FROM A GRATEFUL AUTHOR:

Traveling about, collecting 4-H background material for this book, has been the kind of "work" every writer dreams of. Frankly, I never enjoyed myself more. Everywhere I went I found a cordial welcome and a generous interest in my venture. Of the many new friends I made among 4-H members, leaders, and directors, I would like to express particular appreciation to the following:

Roger E. Regnier, State Club Leader, Manhattan, Kansas

Roberta Anderson, Assistant State 4-H Club Leader, Manhattan, Kansas; formerly Minnesota 4-H Extension worker

Ed Hedstrom, County Agent, Marshall County, Kansas

Ray Zimmerman, Assistant County Agent, Marysville, Kansas

Mrs. Joe Budenbender, Bigelow, Kansas

Rollyn P. Winters, 4-H Extension Leader, New Brunswick, New Jersey

William F. Greenawalt, County Agricultural Agent, Bucks County, Pennsylvania

Frances Vannoy, Extension Home Economist, Bucks County, Pennsylvania

Richard A. Bailey, Assistant County Agent, Bucks County, Pennsylvania

Orville A. Yoder, Assistant County Agent, Bucks County, Pennsylvania

Ben Westrate, Executive Director, 4-H Club Foundation, East Lansing, Michigan

Frank Madaski, County Agent, Hancock, Michigan

Wallace Keskitalo, 4-H Leader, Hancock, Michigan

Dr. E. W. Aiton, Director, 4-H Club Programs, Federal Extension Service, Washington, D.C.

Ellen Winters, New Brunswick, New Jersey

Luella Schroeder, Marysville, Kansas

NOTE FROM A GRATEFUL AUTHOR

Special Information:

Jay Hines, President, Kansas Saddle Horse Association
Joseph Appleby, D.V.M., Scarsdale, New York
Frank Grenci, Fox Hill Farms Stables, Pleasantville, New York
Ellen Edwards Linson, Director of Recreation, Prince George's
  County, Maryland
Elizabeth Edwards Smith, Irvington-on-Hudson, New York

My very special thanks go to the William Edwards family of Bigelow,
Kansas, and the Harold Stump family of Blue Rapids, Kansas. In true
4-H style, parents and children working together, they practically made
a family "project" of this book.

A.C.

Contents

Lucky Four

CHAPTER 1

Homework

It was hot for the last week of September.

"Broiling, roasting, baking hot," Jill Miller thought crossly. Too hot for September and too hot for school—much too hot to be studying homework.

Jill was alone in her room. The last rays of the western sun beat down on the low eaves of the Miller ranch house.

Once the sun had dropped behind the high roof of the barn and beyond the horizon, a breeze would sweep over the Kansas fields that were plowed and ready for the fall wheat planting. But right now not a breath of air stirred.

Jill twisted her blond pony tail in a bun and pinned it up. That made her neck feel cooler. Then she kicked off her dusty sneakers and wiggled her toes. Daddy wouldn't let her go barefooted around the ranch. There were too many rusty nails while they were building the new shed on the barn. The suntan on her toes was left from summer days beside the swimming pool in the Dale Valley Park. Jill and her best friend, Sally Patterson, had really roasted themselves this summer. Jill smiled to herself, remembering how wonderful it had felt to stretch out and broil, first on one side, and then on the other—and then dive into the cold water and listen to their teeth chatter.

One day Scotty, their 4-H county leader, had come along to find the girls at the edge of the pool. "Take it easy, gals," he had said. "Don't overcook yourselves. I could grill a pair of hamburgers on your shoulders right now. You must be trying to store up enough heat to last you through the coldest Kansas winter."

Jill hoped that was true. Hot as she was right now, she shivered to think of winter coming. Other people might mind the blazing Kansas summers, but Jill's older brother, Chuck, had taught her not to.

"Whenever you feel hot," Chuck said, "just shut your eyes and imagine a winter morning when it's still dark and Dad calls you to get up. You put your foot out on the floor—and it's exactly like stepping into a tray of ice cubes! Remember that, Jilly-Dilly, and you'll never complain about a Kansas summer."

Jill stretched her legs out straight and looked at them, hoping they were growing long and slim. Jill was always wishing she were tall, like Sally. Sally's figure was slender. Her clothes looked wonderful on her. Her dark hair was always carefully waved and brushed.

Sometimes Jill looked at herself in the mirror and sighed. "Sally's the glamour gal," she would tell her mother. "I'm just the unmade-bed type. My hair won't stay smooth, and I'll never have a waistline!"

When Jill had been a plump little girl, her father had nicknamed her Jilly-Dilly-Dumpling. Now that she was older, she had learned not to eat too many candy bars and chocolate malts, and she wasn't quite so plump. Her brother Chuck comforted her. "Don't fret, Jilly-Dilly," he said. "It's better to be round than square."

4

"Everyone else in our family was born thin," Jill mourned. "I don't see why *I* had to be the roly-poly."

Jill found too many nice things in life, however, to fret long. Her blue eyes were full of friendliness, and she smiled at people because she liked them. Even the freckles on her nose had a cheerful look.

On this September evening, with a pile of homework to do, Jill certainly had no time to worry about a perfect figure. She tucked her legs under the desk and opened her math book to start work in earnest.

Half an hour later a voice floated up the stairs.

"Ji-ill—"

"Hi!" Jill hurried out to the head of the stairs and looked down on the top of Sally Patterson's sleek, dark head. "Come on up. How did you ever get over on a school night?"

Sally's father's farm was more than a mile away and both families were strict about no visiting on week nights. There was even a limit of twenty minutes on telephone calls, which Sally and Jill agreed was just plain cruel. It scarcely gave them time to say "hello" and "good-by."

The two girls sat down on the bed in Jill's room. "Gosh, I'm glad to see you," Jill said. "I was about to die when I saw that problem in math where we have to figure out how much interest the man paid on the money he borrowed to build a house."

"Cheer up. I've already died over it." Sally leaned back against the pillow. "And don't ask me how to do it. I asked Mom to help me and even she couldn't get the right answer."

Sally's mother was a Home Ec teacher, and both girls regarded her as the last authority on any school subject. "If your mother can't figure it out, there's no use my even trying." Jill sighed. "Maybe they printed the problem wrong in the book."

"Never mind about math right now," Sally went on. "I have something to tell you. Dad came over tonight to talk to your father about a new boy who's come to live at the Marshalls' ranch. Dad went over to see Mr. Marshall on business this afternoon, and he met Alex—that's the new boy's name. Dad thought Alex ought to get into 4-H and join the Merrymakers Club."

Jill nodded. She and Sally and nearly all the other boys and girls they knew had been in 4-H ever since they had been old enough to be members. Both the girls' fathers were club leaders. "Do you mean Alex is going to live at the Marshalls' all the time?" Jill asked. "Or is he just visiting?"

"Well, neither, really," Sally explained. "Dad says Alex's father and mother have gone to Alaska. His father has a job there, but his mother has been sick and they weren't sure they could find a place to live in time for Alex to start school. Mr. Marshall is Alex's uncle, so Alex is coming to live with the Marshalls this year anyway, until his family gets settled in a new home. Alex doesn't know anyone here— and of course he's new in school. So Dad thought the quickest way for Alex to make friends would be to join the Merrymakers. Dad's already talked to Carol about it—"

Jill nodded again. Carol Chase was the president of their 4-H Merrymakers Club this year. Carol was older than Jill and Sally. Ever since Carol's own mother had died, Mrs. Miller and Mrs. Patterson had been second mothers to her. Jill and Sally looked up to Carol like an older sister.

"Dad's asking your father to lend Alex a beef calf or a lamb to start him off with a project," Sally went on.

Jill's thoughts drifted off uncomfortably. Every 4-H member chose some special work to do for a project. Jill had started a dozen projects herself since she had been a 4-H member, but somehow she seldom seemed to finish one. It wasn't that Jill didn't love 4-H. She was as loyal to the Merrymakers Club as anyone and she never missed a meeting. Only when it came to projects, she would start out full of enthusiasm for each new one. Then, before the work was finished, she'd lose interest, or forget to keep her record book up to date, or start off on something new.

More often than Jill liked to remember, Scotty had marked one of her projects *"incomplete."* Her closet and dresser drawers held telltale reminders of her unfinished sewing projects—skirts and blouses with basting threads still in them, dresses without collars or hems. More than once Chuck or Jill's father had taken over a calf or a lamb or chickens when she had given up a project halfway through.

As long as Chuck had been at home, Jill hadn't really minded. Chuck would do the chores she had forgotten, and give her a wink or a grin. Now that Chuck was away at college, it was different. Daddy didn't wink or grin. He just did the work and said nothing, but he put his lips tightly together in a way that could make Jill feel miserable.

Chuck had been a wonderful 4-H member. He had raised everything from pigeons to vegetables, to grain crops and beef calves. He had shown his projects at county and state fairs.

Even Jill's younger sister, Jo Ann, who had been a 4-H member only for a year, had already won a prize for her baking-powder biscuits.

Now that Daddy was their club leader, Jill wished more than ever that she could make him as proud of her as he was of Chuck and Jo Ann. She was determined that this year would be different. She would choose *one* project and really stick to it. The only trouble was that she had changed her mind a dozen times about what her project would be. One day she thought she might redecorate her bedroom, another day she would decide to raise badgers like Gig Williamson— or she'd wonder whether Daddy would let her try a dairy project and raise a heifer.

Jill pulled her thoughts back to the subject of the new boy who was going to join the Merrymakers. "What's he like?" she asked Sally. "The new boy, I mean."

Sally hesitated. "Well—he's nice looking," she said finally. "But there's something kind of—different about him."

"Different how?" Jill was curious.

Sally frowned. "I don't know exactly. Maybe it's just that he looks so unhappy. I think that's why Daddy specially wanted to talk to your father about him. Anyway"—Sally jumped up as she heard her father whistle for her—"Alex is going to be in our math class in school. You'll see him. Maybe you can figure out what makes him different."

CHAPTER 2

The New Boy

The next morning Jill clattered down the stairs later than usual. She held her belt in her teeth. She buttoned her blouse as she skidded around the corner into the kitchen. She was just in time to make a last-minute dab at helping with breakfast.

Jo Ann had already set the table and put out the milk. Now she was buttering toast.

Jill was expected to do more than help her mother. Since Chuck was away, her father needed help with the barn chores. Jill always meant to get out in time to feed the cattle, but she seldom managed to do it. Now, after all her good resolutions, here she was late again. There was no time to do anything but to take the plates of scrambled eggs her mother handed her and put them on the table.

Jill sat down quickly, feeling cross at everyone. "It isn't fair of Mommy and Daddy always to be so patient," she told herself resentfully. "If they'd just get mad and punish me, I'd be better."

It was a relief to Jill when her father came to the table and they began to talk about Alex Marshall. The new boy was coming to the Merrymakers' meeting that evening, Mr.

Miller said. "It's up to you members to tell Alex what 4-H is all about," he went on. "Sally's father says Alex has never belonged to a club. In fact, he'd never heard of 4-H before."

"*Never heard of 4-H?*" Jo Ann put down her spoon and faced her father indignantly. "That's silly! Everybody in America has heard of 4-H, Daddy."

"Not quite, I'm afraid." Mr. Miller smiled. "There are 4-H clubs all over the country, but most of them are in farming neighborhoods like ours. You youngsters have been born and raised 4-H. But there are plenty of towns and cities—like the one where Alex lived—where there aren't any 4-H clubs at all."

"Well, then"—Jo Ann went back to her oatmeal—"I just feel awfully sorry for people who live in places like that."

"Then do your best to make Alex feel at home tonight." Mr. Miller smiled again. "From what Sally's father tells me, I don't think the boy is very happy here so far."

Jill said nothing. She had gulped down her cereal and eggs. Now she hurried to gather up her books, hunt for a missing page of her English composition, and slap together a sandwich for her school lunch. She popped an apple and a slice of cheese into the bag and scooped up her books. "Bye, Mom. Bye, Daddy," she called over her shoulder, and raced after Jo Ann down the road toward the highway. She was just in time to climb up into the school bus.

Sally had saved her seat. Jill sat down with a sigh of relief. Now that she was away from home it was easy to forget how cross she had felt a few minutes before. The noisy, cheerful hum of voices in the bus made it impossible to think about anything serious.

"Gosh"—Jill breathed to Sally, smoothing back her hair

and pulling her pony tail tighter—"I thought I'd never make it this morning!"

In math class that morning Jill caught her first glimpse of the new boy. Sally nudged her arm as a tall figure came through the door. "That's Alex," Sally whispered.

Jill turned to see the boy drop into one of the back seats. He was good looking, as Sally had said. His light hair was crew-cut close to his head. His eyes were deep gray. His head was already bent over the book in front of him.

During class, Jill glanced around again two or three times, but Alex was always staring at his book.

"I guess Alex isn't very anxious to make friends," Jill told Sally later. "He won't even look at anyone."

Jill had English the first period after lunch. It was her favorite class, and Miss Bailey was her favorite teacher. They were reading *The Merchant of Venice*, and Miss Bailey asked Jill to take the part of Portia when they read the trial scene.

Jill loved to act. When she stepped in front of the class, she forgot everything except Shakespeare's dramatic words:

"The quality of mercy is not strain'd,
   It droppeth as the gentle rain from heaven
   Upon the place beneath: it is twice bless'd;
   It blesseth him that gives and him that takes. . . ."

At the end of class Miss Bailey said, "You read very well, Jill—with real feeling. Why don't you try out for the school play we're giving after the game on Homecoming Weekend? Here's a copy of the play. There are several parts you can try for."

The play was *Our Town*.

Jill had been to the movie of *Our Town* and she had seen the play on TV. But she read the lines over that afternoon, in her room at home, and they seemed more beautiful than anything she remembered.

Miss Bailey hadn't said which parts Jill was to try for. When she came to the last scene, in the cemetery, Jill read Emily's lines to herself, and she felt a prickle of excitement creep up her spine. Emily was the leading part—of course, one of the older girls would be sure to get it. Probably Kathy Donaldson, who was a senior, and the best actress in school. But suppose she tried out for the part anyway, Jill asked herself? And suppose—just suppose Miss Bailey chose her to play it?

Jill remembered something Miss Bailey had once said to her. "You have plenty of ability, Jill. You could do good work if there were something you really wanted to work for. I guess we've all heard of the Jack-of-all-trades"—Miss Bailey had smiled—"but you're a Jill-of-all-trades. You can do too many things well, Jill. Someday you'll have to choose just one to *work* on—one you really care about. Then we'll be proud of you!"

She'd really care about this, Jill thought. If only she had the chance to play Emily's part, she would show Miss Bailey how hard she could work.

She'd start working right now. In a burst of ambition, Jill sat down at her desk and attacked her homework for the next day. She flew through her history and English assignments and finished her math in time to dash out to the barn just as her father was starting his evening chores.

"Hi, Daddy," Jill called out a trifle breathlessly. "Any jobs for me?"

Mr. Miller gave no sign of surprise. He had seen enough

of Jill's sudden fits of energy to take them calmly. He may have wondered what caused the sparkle of excitement in her eyes this time, but he only said matter-of-factly, "Well, you could mix the grain for the calves," and handed her a measure. "Then you could get some hay down from the loft."

Jill mixed and measured the grain and spread it on the feeding trough. "Come on, boys"—she gave the nearest steer a push—"soup's on!" The big steer lumbered toward the trough and the other calves, coming in from the field, crowded around and started eating noisily.

Pitching down bales from the hayloft, Jill glanced over at the old sack-swing that hung from the barn's highest rafter. It was a long time since Jill had taken a swing. She thought what fun it would be to swoop the length of the long barn and back.

Jill remembered how Chuck had helped her take her first swing years ago, and how scared she had been. He had showed her how to take a tight grip on the rope, then wrap her legs around the folded sack seat.

Jill remembered saying in a small voice, "I'm afraid I'll look down—and I'll be so scared I'll let go."

"Keep your eyes shut," Chuck had said firmly. "Then you can't look down." And he had given her the first push.

Jill had looked down anyway. It seemed miles to the barn floor below. But she hadn't let go. After the first breathless *whoosh* she felt as though she had been flying through space all her life.

Now, however, Jill looked sternly away from the swing and went on heaving down hay bales, remembering her new determination to work hard. She even offered to feed the chickens, a chore she particularly disliked. And every moment she worked, she was thinking of the play and how wonderful it would be if she could even hope for the leading part.

Helping her mother put dinner on the table, Jill moved around the kitchen, already imagining herself playing the part of Emily in the first act. She was quite lost in her performance when she realized suddenly that her mother and Jo Ann were staring at her.

"Jill, answer your sister," her mother said.

Jill stared blankly. She hadn't heard a word.

"I asked you three times," Jo Ann said, speaking very slowly and distinctly, "whether I could borrow your red cardigan to wear to the Merrymakers' meeting tonight. Please?"

"Oh—" Jill came back from *Our Town* with a thud. She had forgotten all about the 4-H meeting. "Oh sure, Jo-Jo. It's in my closet. Help yourself."

"Thanks," Jo Ann said. But on her way to the door she gave Jill a last curious glance. "Were you hearing voices or something?" she asked.

On the way to the 4-H meeting that evening, Jill sat in the back seat of the car, between Sally and Alex. Jo Ann and Sally's brother, Jerry, were in front with Mr. Miller.

"Remember, it's up to you girls to tell Alex something about 4-H," Jill's father said over his shoulder, "so he'll know what he's getting into before he joins the Merrymakers."

Sally and Jill started in enthusiastically. They bombarded Alex with information, interrupting each other with every other sentence as they explained to Alex that there were 4-H clubs in every state in America and in other countries, too. "They even have 4-H in Japan and South America and lots of places in Europe," Sally said earnestly.

"And there's a 4-H Congress every year," Jill put in. "With boys and girls who are members from everywhere in the world. They come from all sorts of different places, but they all believe we ought to be *friends*—and they all work on different projects. ..."

"What are projects?" Alex asked. He was listening politely enough, but his voice sounded as though he were quite sure he wouldn't like projects, whatever they were.

"Oh, good grief! There are dozens and dozens of them." The girls looked at each other and started counting. "There are poultry projects, and fat lambs, and vegetable gardens, and cooking and sewing and beef calves—" Sally rattled off the list.

"And there are dairy projects, and pigs, and grain crops, and forestry," Jill continued, "and raising bees and running tractors and decorating rooms. ..."

"Don't forget my rabbits," Jo Ann put in, from the front seat, as her sister paused for breath.

"And that's not nearly all," Jill finished. "Gig Williamson started raising badgers as a project last year. The very first season he earned enough money selling pelts to help his father put a new roof on the barn. And Tim Stanford raises quail."

"I guess almost anything a 4-H member wanted to do could be a project," Sally said, "if Scotty thought it was worth while."

"Scotty's our Dale County 4-H agent," Jill explained. "Every county has one. And—"

"*Whoa-a!* Slow down." Alex put up his hands. "I'm all

15

mixed up. *Projects, counties, 4-H agents.* I can't keep it straight!"

"Take it easy, gals," Mr. Miller said, laughing. "Remember—you've been 4-H members since you were ten years old. Don't expect Alex to know everything you do in one evening."

"Well, you told us to tell him," Jill protested. "Anyway, anyone can learn to have fun in one evening. And Merrymakers' meetings are certainly fun!"

CHAPTER 3

Merrymakers' Meeting

The Merrymakers' clubhouse was an abandoned one-room school just off the highway. Every so often, during the summer, the Merrymaker boys came over to mow down the grass in front of the little old school. But the Kansas sun always got ahead of them. By the end of summer the grass and weeds had grown so tall that the members had to wade knee-high to reach the door.

The old schoolhouse had only one large, square room. The building was made of sturdy brick, but when the Merry-makers met, the walls sometimes seemed to bulge with the noise and laughter of the group inside.

There was no age limit in the Merrymakers. Mothers and fathers of 4-H members came to the meeting, and they brought their younger children. The babies slept on their mothers' laps. The little boys and girls played at a sandbox in the corner of the room while the meeting went on.

This evening Jill found herself sitting next to Alex. She leaned over to explain one last thing to him. "Our club is called the Merrymakers," she said, "but all the clubs have different names—like the Hustlers and the Wide Awakes, and the Sunflowers and the Buttons and Bows—oh, there are heaps."

Alex nodded politely.

I wish he'd smile just once, Jill thought. Or frown. Or something. Then I'd have some idea what he's thinking.

As the meeting was called to order, the room grew quiet. Even the smallest children, who were playing at the sandbox, hushed their voices to whispers.

Carol Chase, the Merrymakers' president, raised her hand to lead them in the 4-H pledge.

> *"I pledge my Head to clearer thinking,*
> *My Heart to greater loyalty,*
> *My Hands to larger service, and*
> *My Health to better living,*
>   *for my club, my community, and my country."*

Jill repeated the words with the others. As many times as she had said them, it always made her feel a little solemn when she thought of the thousands and thousands of other 4-H members who were saying the same words. This time, however, she stole a glance at Alex out of the corner of her eye. She wondered whether the words meant anything to him, but there was no way of guessing. He stood looking straight ahead. His expression was serious, yet there was something guarded in his face. Jill had an odd feeling about Alex. As if he had closed a door on things—maybe to shut himself in, or shut other people out. Jill couldn't be sure which.

Carol began to speak, and Jill looked back. Carol ran the meeting smoothly. She called for minutes and asked Tom Briggs, the treasurer, for his report. Tom struggled through a sheaf of pages scribbled with figures, and finally wound up a little desperately, "I can't tell exactly how much money we have, because every time I add it up it comes out a different answer. But, anyway, I think we're O.K., Carol—I mean, Madam President." Tommy sat down to a burst of laughter and applause.

Next, plans were suggested for taking Thanksgiving baskets to the Dale Valley Hospital patients and for a carol sing in the hospital on Christmas Eve. Then Tim Stanford and Gig Williamson, both wearing red stocking caps, and toting guns, gave a demonstration of safety rules for hunters.

Jill saw Johnny Lane sitting in a seat against the back wall. She saw that his eyes never left Carol's face. Johnny had been a 4-H member as long as Jill's brother Chuck had been. Johnny was in his last year of college now, but whenever he was at home, he still came to the Merrymakers' meetings. They all knew that the one thing in the world Johnny wanted most was to be a doctor. And Jill knew that it was Carol who had encouraged him the most. Carol wanted to be a nurse herself. Johnny was watching Carol as she stood straight and slim behind the desk, her honey-blond hair shining, her smile gentle. When Johnny looked at Carol like that, Jill thought, he might have been looking at a star in the sky—a star that was very far away, very beautiful and steady.

Jill sighed. Ever since she had been a little girl, she had looked up to Carol and wanted to be like her. She had told Chuck that once, and he just laughed. "Jilly-Dilly, you'll never be like Carol in a million years. Why don't you just relax and enjoy being *you?*"

One of Jill's earliest memories was when she had been a little girl, and Chuck had been furious because she had spoiled his first 4-H demonstration. Jill had been playing at the sand table, where the little ones played now, and she had let out a loud howl when another little girl grabbed her favorite yellow shovel.

"I just can't go on being in 4-H if you bring that brat to meetings," Chuck had complained bitterly to his father and mother later. He had pointed accusingly at Jill.

But Jill remembered that when she had stumbled through her own first demonstration as a 4-H member, Chuck had clapped loudly in the audience.

Being in 4-H was as familiar to Jill as being in her own family, or in church. Yet tonight she looked around the room and her mind was full of questions. Maybe it was just wanting to be in the school play so badly that made her feel restless. But when she saw Johnny and Carol both so sure of the things they wanted, Jill wondered whether she would ever be as sure of anything as they were. Right this minute she wanted the part of Emily more than anything. But next week or next month or next year, she'd be wanting something entirely different. Sometimes Jill hoped she could be a singer and sometimes she dreamed of being a nurse like Carol, or a teacher, like Sally wanted to be. Other times she just wanted to be married and have children, unless she decided to write books and travel all over the world. But which thing did she *really* want? Which would ever make her feel as sure as Johnny and Carol and Sally felt?

Carol's words brought Jill's attention back to the meeting again.

The Merrymakers had received a letter, Carol was saying, from a boy named Kenny Graham. Kenny lived in a big city in Michigan, and he had been a patient in the hospital Carol had visited last summer and where she hoped to go to study nursing. Carol read the letter aloud.

Dear Merrymakers,

I hope you don't mind my writing to you. When Carol visited here last summer she told about your 4-H club and how hard you work on your projects.

There are 4-H clubs in some cities here, but none in the city where I live. Carol told me how you work on projects, and I have been working on a project by myself since I came home from the hospital. It is plant culture.

I would like to work outdoors, but my family lives in an apartment on the fourth floor of a building, and the doctor says I cannot go up and down stairs just yet. So my dad helped me make a window-box garden where I can experiment. I get books from the library to study about plants, and I have been working especially with rye and barley. I have tried crossing different varieties to get a plant that gives more grain.

Now I need some help, to find out how my seeds will grow as outdoor crops. Carol wrote me that some of the Merrymakers are working on grain projects. Would you be willing to plant the seeds I am sending, and let me know how the plants turn out? If you think my seeds give plants with better grain, I will be glad to send you more next season.

Very truly yours, with thanks,
KENNY GRAHAM

Carol looked at Tim Stanford when she finished reading. "Tim," Carol asked, "would you and the others who are working on grain projects be willing to plant Kenny's seeds and send him reports?"

"Oh, sure." Tim took the box that Carol handed him and

looked at the bags of seeds packed inside, each one carefully tagged. He read a few labels and whistled admiringly. "This kid really knows his stuff," Tim said. "Sure, we'll plant Kenny's seeds and write him how the grain turns out."

"Wait a minute, Carol, I have a better idea." Gig Williamson suddenly unfolded his long legs and stood up. "Why can't we invite Kenny to visit here next spring? Then he could see how his seeds are growing, and he could really be outdoors and have some fun—" Gig stopped, remembering the club rules. He straightened his shoulders and said seriously, "Madam President, I move we invite Kenny Graham to visit the Merrymakers, if he can come."

"I second the motion," Jo Ann said. "And I think it would be a wonderful idea. If Kenny still isn't supposed to walk much, we could drive him around. We could drive him right onto the fields to see the grain crops, and into the barns to see our animal projects."

The motion was carried unanimously, and the meeting adjourned with everyone talking about what fun it would be to have Kenny come and visit.

Carol promised to write a letter to invite him.

After the meeting, brownies and cookies and bottles of soda were served.

Jill found herself standing next to Alex. She was trying to explain about 4-H leaders, who were usually parents, and the junior leaders, who were chosen from the older boys and girls in the clubs. "The junior leaders help the younger members with projects," Jill told Alex. "Carol has been a junior leader for three years. Sally will probably be one next year. She'll work with the 4-H'rs who have baby-beef projects. That's Sally's specialty. She raises the calves to sell, and she's saving the money to go to college. Her father helps by giving her a new calf from his herd every year."

Alex glanced at Jill. "What's your specialty?" he asked. He didn't sound really interested.

"Oh, I don't know—" Jill hesitated. She wished she had a specialty to name. But she was too honest to pretend. "I guess my trouble is that I like too many things," she admitted. "So I never learn much about any of them."

Jill looked up with a smile, but Alex didn't smile back. He was looking off toward the other side of the room as though he hadn't heard her answer.

After refreshments, Mr. Miller had a new game for the Merrymakers to try. He put two pennies on a boy's elbow. "Now let's see you shake them off and catch them with the same hand," he ordered.

They all took turns trying the stunt. But when Mr. Miller handed the pennies to Alex, the boy shook his head.

"No thanks. I'll just watch," Alex said.

They dropped Alex at the Marshalls' farm on the way home. After they left him, the girls were quiet for a few minutes.

Then Sally gave a long sigh. "Well, we certainly tried to make Alex have a good time, just like we promised," she burst out. "Only what can you do when a person just won't make friends or have fun?"

"I know you girls did your best," Mr. Miller said. "But don't give up yet. Remember, this is all new to Alex. He never heard of 4-H or met any of you until tonight."

There was another silence. Then Jill said suddenly, a little defiantly, "Well, I asked Alex to the barbecue on Saturday and he said he'd come."

The Millers had a family barbecue every Saturday noon as long as the good weather lasted, and the children were always welcome to invite their friends.

"Oh, *no*," Sally groaned. "Honestly, Jill, why did you? He'll just be a wet blanket again." She shrugged. "If you want to be noble, O.K.—but don't expect me to help."

"*I'll* help," Jo Ann spoke up unexpectedly. "I like Alex. I'll show him my rabbits."

"Good for you, Jo-Jo." Mr. Miller nodded. "And good for you too, Jill."

"But I wasn't being noble," Jill said. "I asked Alex because—" she hesitated. Then she gave up with a laugh. "Oh, maybe because he's different—and I'm just curious."

Next morning in math class, when Alex barely glanced up to say "hello," Jill began to wonder why she had asked him to the barbecue.

Maybe he won't come, she told herself. Maybe he'll forget.

But Jill's next class was English and when Miss Bailey announced that tryouts for the school play would be next Monday, it drove every other thought from Jill's mind.

CHAPTER **4**

Barbecue

Alex didn't forget Jill's invitation.

He appeared at the Miller ranch on Saturday, in blue jeans and a neat white shirt. During lunch he was quiet. He sat stiffly at the edge of the group.

Jill caught a martyred glance from Sally. "I *told* you he'd be a wet blanket," Sally's look said.

But when Jo Ann invited Alex to come and see her rabbits he went readily enough, and Jo Ann came back to whisper encouragingly in Jill's ear: "Alex was *nice*, Dilly, just like I said. And he loved my rabbits. He remembered every single name the first time. He's not nearly as bashful with animals."

When Jill showed Alex around the ranch later, she understood what Jo Ann meant. As long as they were looking at the calves and the sheep, patting Cindy, the shepherd collie, inspecting the latest litter of barn kittens, Alex seemed at ease. He even made a few friendly clucks at the chickens, although Jill had never imagined that anyone could feel really personal about a chicken.

But when they turned a corner into the west pasture, and Alex saw the two horses, his face really came to life. He walked over to Laddie, the palomino, and put out his hand. "Hello there, boy. Hello, fellow," he said softly.

Jill watched curiously. Alex's whole manner changed as he stroked the palomino's neck. For the first time the odd, guarded look was gone from Alex's eyes. Then he walked over to Dolly, the little quarter-horse mare.

"I didn't know you had such good horses," Alex said.

"We don't always," Jill answered. "Daddy just happened to bring these two back after the last fair. A friend of his, in the next county, was selling his ranch and wanted to get rid of them. The mare was in foal, and Daddy thought it would be too bad to let her go to a dealer. He thought Jo-Jo and I could ride Laddie"—Jill paused and shook her head at the palomino—"but he just won't *be* ridden. Every time we try, Laddie kicks and bucks until we've just about given up."

Alex frowned. "Maybe it's not Laddie's fault," he said. "He could be lame, you know."

"All the time?" Jill asked.

"Sure, if there were something really wrong." Alex was bending down, feeling the horse's legs carefully. When he touched one hind foot, the palomino shot out a quick kick. Alex didn't jump back. He tried the foot again more gently.

"That could be your trouble right there," Alex said. "If a horse has a bad leg it can make him just about impossible to ride, especially if he doesn't get the right treatment. Anyway"—he stood up—"don't go blaming Laddie for something that's probably not his fault at all."

"You'd better tell Daddy," Jill said. "I heard him say the other day that he just didn't know what to do about Laddie." She looked at Alex curiously. "How did you learn so much about horses?"

"Just being around them." Alex shrugged. "I've known horses ever since I can remember. They're the nicest animals in the world to work with—if they're treated right. And they're the easiest ones to spoil with bad care. I had a horse, Charger—" Alex stopped speaking suddenly, as though he had said more than he meant to. He bent his head quickly over Laddie's foot again. "But that was a long time ago," he finished abruptly.

Jill was more curious than ever. She was just going to ask what had happened to Charger, when she looked down and stopped short as she saw Alex's hands. They were doubled into fists, so tightly that the knuckles showed white. And Jill saw that they were trembling.

She bit back the question about Charger. "I—I suppose we ought to get back to the house," she said instead. "Daddy wants to drive into Dale Valley to see about some 4-H business, and Sally and I promised to go with him."

Walking back, Alex looked at Jill for a moment. "This 4-H really means a lot to you, doesn't it?" he said.

"Oh, I guess I'm the same about 4-H as you are about horses." Jill smiled. "I've always been around 4-H. Daddy and Mother met each other at a conference when they were both 4-H leaders a long time ago. Chuck and Jo-Jo and I were just naturally born 4-H."

Driving into Dale Valley later that afternoon, Jill told Sally about showing Alex the ranch. "Jo-Jo was right," she said. "Alex is twice as nice with animals as he is with people. He wants to talk to Daddy about Laddie. I think he's even going to ask Daddy to let him try to train Laddie."

"Well, I'm glad Alex is human about something, even if it's only animals." Sally sighed.

"Especially horses." Jill nodded. For a moment she was going on to say that Alex had once had a horse of his own, named Charger. Then she remembered how suddenly Alex had stopped speaking, and how she had looked down to see his fists doubled so tightly.

Somehow it didn't seem right to tell that—even to Sally.

On the morning of the tryouts for the school play Jill scarcely touched her breakfast.

"You haven't eaten enough to keep a chipmunk alive," her mother said, frowning at Jill's plate. "At least drink your milk."

"Mom, I just can't." Jill tried one sip of milk and put the glass down shuddering. "I don't think chipmunks drink milk, anyway. And our hygiene teacher says that if you eat when you're nervous the food just makes a lump in your stomach, or something. Actresses never eat anything before a performance. I read that somewhere."

"M'mm." Her father cleared his throat. "It seems to me I read somewhere that it takes quite a bit of training and experience to make an actress. In other words, I'm not sure that you're entitled to have lumps in your stomach just yet. Let's see that milk go down the hatch, young lady."

For a moment Jill tried to look dignified and wounded and dramatic. But when Jo Ann and her mother laughed heartlessly, Jill gave up and giggled. She gulped the milk in three huge swallows, snatched up her books and lunch, and raced for the door. "All right, if I get a stomach-ache and die on the stage, you'll know whose fault it is!" she called back.

On the school bus Sally patted Jill's arm loyally. "I

know you're going to do just beautifully. I'll bet anything you'll get the part of Emily."

"I couldn't possibly." Jill shook her head. "Kathy Donaldson's sure to get it. She's the best actress in the school. Or, anyway, one of the older girls will get it." She patted her tummy, wondering how many lumps were gathering, and sighed. She had been saying for the past week that there wasn't the smallest chance of getting the Emily part. Still, she couldn't help feeling a little nervous jump every time she thought of it.

The moment Jill stepped out on the platform after assembly to begin reading, she forgot about nervous jumps. She forgot this was the school auditorium, she forgot that Miss Bailey, sitting alone, was her only audience. She forgot the whispering murmur from backstage, where the others were waiting to try out. She only knew that she had to be *Emily*, and she put her whole heart into the lines.

When she had finished reading, Jill went back and sat down. She didn't know whether she had done well or not. She didn't even look at Miss Bailey until the others had finished reading. Then she saw Miss Bailey coming toward her.

"I don't know whether I ought to do this or not, Jill," Miss Bailey began slowly, "but I'd like to let you try the part of Emily."

As Jill started to jump up, her eyes shining, Miss Bailey put her hand out quickly. "Wait a minute," she said warningly. "I'm only asking you to try the part, Jill. It will mean a lot of work and studying."

"Oh, I'll work, I'll study, I'll do anything if you'll just give me the chance," Jill broke in. "I promise."

"All right," Miss Bailey said, "I'll let you try the part."

As Jill dashed off down the hall to tell her friends the wonderful news, Miss Bailey's eyes followed her doubtfully. She was sure Jill could play the part, but would she be willing to work for it? Miss Bailey wondered.

There was no doubt in Jill's mind. She skimmed through the rest of the day on wings. In history class, in gym, even in math class, she seemed to hear nothing but the lines of the play echoing through her mind.

At lunch Jill sat staring into the distance and chewing a mouthful of peanut-butter sandwich until Jane McDougall snapped her fingers in front of Jill's nose. "Hey, come down to earth," Jane said. "This is the lunchroom. You know, that place where we eat lunch. Where were you? Cloud nine?"

"Cloud 109," Jill said, "and it was pink, too." Her face broke into a sudden grin.

The moment Jill flew in the door that afternoon, she told her mother she had a chance for the leading part in the play.

Mrs. Miller was thrilled. She gave Jill a hug. "We'll have to write Chuck about this," she said. "He'll be so pleased."

Jo Ann beamed at her older sister. "Everybody was talking about Jill in school today," she told her mother. "Wait till Daddy hears."

Jill was touched by the look of pride in Jo-Jo's face. She felt a quick moment of remorse for all the times she had sworn that little sisters were nothing but nuisances.

Dinnertime came; still the station wagon hadn't turned in the drive. Mr. Miller was usually home long before this.

Jill watched at the window until finally her mother said,

"Something must be keeping Daddy. We may as well go ahead and eat."

They were halfway through the meal when Mr. Miller came in. He told them he had stopped at the Marshalls' on the way home. "Ed Marshall wanted to talk to me about Alex," Mr. Miller said. "He's been worried about the boy. Alex doesn't make any trouble, Ed says, but he keeps too much to himself. Ed's afraid the boy misses his family more than he lets on. It seems that ever since Alex has started working with Laddie, he talks of nothing but the horse. Ed had an idea that if we let Alex have Laddie, he might take over the horse as a project for 4-H. It's the first interest the boy has shown in 4-H or anything else, Ed says. Ed says he talked to Scotty about it. Scotty says Jerry Patterson wants to start a 4-H horse project, too. The two boys might get a horse group going and get some other Merrymakers interested. I said I'd be willing—especially because Ed thought it would help Alex. But I said I'd have to ask Jill and Jo-Jo first. After all, I really took Laddie for you girls to ride. How about it? Would you be willing to lend Laddie to Alex?"

Jo Ann agreed enthusiastically.

Jill nodded. "I suppose we might as well," she said. "Laddie hasn't really done us any good." She didn't mean to be unfriendly about Alex. Still, she couldn't help feeling disappointed at not having had a chance to tell Daddy her great news right away.

When Mrs. Miller told him about the play later, Daddy was as pleased as the others had been. But somehow even his warm congratulations left Jill feeling a little unsatisfied.

"It isn't anything to get excited about," she said. "After all, it's just a school play. And Miss Bailey says I may not even get the part for sure."

"I know you will, though," Jo Ann said earnestly.

While their father went to telephone Mr. Marshall and make arrangements for Alex to take Laddie, Jo Ann helped Jill clear the table.

"I'll tell you what, Jill," Jo Ann said. "I'll take your turn in doing the dishes tonight so you can start studying your part for the play."

CHAPTER 5

Run Sheep Run

The last week in October the Merrymakers were busy getting their animals ready for the Junior Livestock show in Wichita.

The winning 4-H sheep and hogs and calves from every county in the state would be there, fattened up and groomed to show their best.

Mr. Miller and Mr. Patterson looked over the Merrymakers' entries the night before they left. All of them had won blue ribbons at the Dale County Fair. "But don't forget they'll be up against stiff competition," Mr. Miller said. "Kansas has some mighty fine junior showmen."

Jill went over to watch Sally's two calves, Fat Stuff and Hot Stuff, loaded onto the truck for the trip. Both calves had taken blue ribbons at the County Fair, and Fat Stuff had won the Reserve Championship at the State Fair. Sally had worked until the last minute to get them in perfect shape for the big show in Wichita.

Jill felt as proud as Sally did when she watched Fatty and Hotty lumber up the ramp into the truck. "They're beautiful," Jill said. "I just know they'll win."

"Oh, Jill, I wish you were going, too," Sally said. "Why didn't you finish your calf project this year?"

Jill could only shake her head, remembering the Black Angus calf her father had given her the year before. She had named him Tater Chips and started out ambitiously. But she had left more and more chores undone, until finally Daddy had to take Tater Chips back.

"I guess I'm the only failure in the Miller family." Jill sighed. "Anyway, I'll try again next year." She gave Sally a last good-by hug. "I promise to do better. Then we can go to Wichita together." U. S. 1466657

Jill had no time to be disappointed at not going to the Wichita show. Rehearsals for the school play kept her too busy.

The first week Jill was thrilled every moment she was on the stage. She loved the play and she loved her part. She tried to follow every word of Miss Bailey's direction. By the end of the week, however, it began to seem less exciting to go over and over the same lines. Several times Jill found herself fidgeting impatiently while Miss Bailey explained just how a scene should go.

When Miss Bailey asked Jill whether she wanted to go on with the part, however, Jill was still enthusiastic. "Remember, this is a hard part to play," Miss Bailey warned her. "I'd intended to give the part to Kathy Donaldson, because she's our most experienced actress. But it was Kathy who asked me to give you the chance. Kathy has had so many leading parts, she wanted you to have this one. If you think it's too hard, just tell me."

"Oh, no, Miss Bailey." Jill shook her head. "It isn't one bit too hard. And I love the part. Please let me go on."

"All right." Miss Bailey patted Jill's arm. "Work hard

over the weekend. I expect the first-act lines memorized by Monday."

Jill went home determined to study her lines all Saturday and Sunday.

She did study Saturday morning. Then the Merrymakers came home from Wichita, and Jill forgot about learning lines in the excitement of hearing what had happened.

Sally was beaming. She had sold Fat Stuff and Hot Stuff for good prices. "Every penny I put in the bank gets me nearer to college," Sally told Jill. Sally's ambition was to be a teacher, like her mother.

The other Merrymakers had done well. Jerry Patterson had a prize for one of his hogs. Lois Hanson brought the Merrymakers their highest honor. One of her Hampshire lambs had won a blue ribbon.

There was a party at the Miller ranch that evening to celebrate.

A picnic supper of baked beans, hamburgers, and potato salad was set out. Mrs. Miller had baked pans of hot rolls that smelled delicious. And Jo Ann made angel-food cake for dessert.

Jill helped her father bring bales of hay from the barn and put them in a circle, for the guests to sit on.

Then they built a high bonfire in the center.

It was a perfect evening, mild and clear. As they finished eating supper, the round harvest moon came up behind the high barn roof.

"Everybody ready for a swing," Mr. Miller called. "Let's go!"

Jill stood beside Alex while he watched the younger ones on the sack swing. They flew across the barn, from one end to the other, squealing with excitement. "If you think this is scary, wait till you see them do a sack swing in the dark," Jill told Alex.

After supper Mr. Miller suggested a game of Run Sheep Run. They divided into teams, with a captain for each. After one team had hidden, the other team went to hunt for them.

Jill was on the first team. They found a hiding place under the chute where the cattle were sent down for branding. There they huddled, crowded together, hardly daring to breathe, while they waited for their captain to call signals they had decided on. Names of soft drinks meant "look out, they're coming toward you." Names of ice-cream flavors meant "you're safe."

Jill crouched with the others, listening for the signals. When they heard their captain call "Peppermint stick, vanilla, chocolate chip," they kept quiet, knowing they were safe.

Suddenly the signals changed. "Pepi-Cola," the captain called. "Coca-Cola, cherry soda, 7-Up, ORANGE POP."

The team that was hiding braced itself. They knew the enemy was near. "Ginger ale," the captain shouted, and then "RUN SHEEP RUN."

They raced for the home base and landed in a breathless, laughing heap.

"We won!"

"No, *we* won!"

Both teams shouted together.

"You *all* won," Mr. Miller said. "Come on, we'll play again."

After the second game, the younger children went back for a last wild round on the sack swing in the barn. "The young fry don't think it's really exciting until they can dare each other to make the swing in the pitch dark," Mr. Miller explained to Alex.

The others gathered around the circle again, glad enough to rest and watch the fire. Presently someone began to hum the 4-H Field Song, and they took up the words:

> *"Sing for the wide, wide fields*
> *Sing for the wide, wide sky*
> *Sing for the good, glad earth . . ."*

Then they drifted into "Home on the Range," and finally, softly, "Swing Low, Sweet Chariot."

Jill looked across the circle at Alex. She hoped that he was beginning to feel more at home with the Merrymakers. She hoped he was happier, now that Daddy had given him Laddie to take care of.

Alex joined in the singing. He had played in the games earlier. But as he sat staring into the fire, there was no way to guess what thoughts lay behind the sober expression in his gray eyes.

The harvest moon rode high, round and golden, when they all said good-night.

Jill stood with her family, waving good-by as the last cars drove away. They went into the house together. After all the noise and voices, everything seemed hushed and quiet.

The fire, in the circle outside, had died down to a bed of embers that glowed gently in the darkness.

Jill was almost asleep before she remembered that she hadn't spent a single minute studying her part for the play.

CHAPTER 6

Last Rehearsal

Rehearsal on Monday was misery for Jill. All the others had learned their lines for the first act, while she could only stumble through her part, waiting for Miss Bailey to prompt her on nearly every speech.

Jill studied frantically that night. But the next rehearsal was no better, nor the next. No matter how hard she studied, the others were always ahead of her. Jill's part was the longest one in the play. She had waited too long before she settled down to working on it.

By the end of the week everyone was discouraged. After the Friday rehearsal Jill knew she would never be able to catch up with the others. She walked off the stage, not looking at anyone, and sat down.

It was almost a relief when Miss Bailey came over and said kindly, "Jill, I'm sorry. I'm afraid I'll have to put Kathy in as Emily. I warned you this would be a hard part—maybe I was wrong to let you try it. You read the lines so well in the tryout I wanted to give you a chance. But we have such a short time to finish rehearsing before Homecoming Weekend—"

As Jill nodded and turned away, Miss Bailey put out her

hand. "Please don't give up, Jill. You have real talent for acting. Try again next year. Only try harder."

Jill nodded once more. She even managed to smile back at Miss Bailey. When the others in the cast crowded around to tell her how sorry they were, she still managed to look cheerful. Kathy Donaldson put her arm around Jill. "I won't do half as well as you could have done," Kathy said.

Jill was out of the auditorium and halfway down the hall when someone called her name, and she turned to see Alex. She had forgotten that Alex had volunteered as one of the stage-lighting crew. Of course he had seen what had just happened. Jill stiffened herself for another sympathetic comment. But there was nothing sympathetic about Alex's expression. His gray eyes, which were usually so cool, blazed straight at Jill. He took a long breath. Suddenly he blurted out, "For Pete's sake, Jill, you were good in that part. You were really *dumb* to lose it."

For a moment Jill was too surprised to do anything. Her cheeks turned as red as though Alex had actually slapped her. Even as anger boiled up in her, Jill realized a strange thing. Alex had said a mean thing, but he didn't look mean. His eyes met Jill's levelly. She didn't remember Alex ever looking straight at her before. His eyes were filled with real distress.

Still, it was more than Jill could bear to be spoken to like that. Before she could stop herself, she flung angry words back at him, "Oh, mind your own business! And let me get by—"

The moment Jill had spoken, she would have given anything to take the words back. But it was too late. She pushed past Alex, but not quickly enough to see what her words had done.

Something in Alex's eyes went off like a light. The guarded look came over his face again. His mouth tightened in a straight line as he swung out of her way and went off without another word.

Quite suddenly, Jill felt something happening to her. Something coming up like a lump in her thoat. She ducked down the hall and into the locker room just in time, before the tears spilled down her cheeks.

Luckily the room was empty. Jill dabbed at her eyes furiously. She wasn't used to tears. Her mother always said, "Jill is the one who never cries."

Now she was crying, helplessly, with long, deep sobs that came from so deep inside her she couldn't swallow them back. "Darn," she whispered between the racking breaths. "Darn, *darn.*"

It was bad enough to be crying—but even worse not to know what she was crying for.

Was it only because she had failed in the play? Or because of what Alex had said? Or the way she had answered him? Why should she keep remembering the way Alex had looked at her—as though, in spite of his words, he really cared about her losing the part? Or was she just tired, after the week of struggling through rehearsals?

The storm tore through her as though it would never stop. All the mistakes she had made in her whole life seemed to come flooding back in that moment.

And then it was past. Jill pulled herself up straight. She went over to the basin and splashed cold water on her face. She ran a comb through her hair and fluffed out her pony tail. Dabbing her nose with powder, she glared at herself in the mirror. *"All right, so you're a failure,"* she told herself, gritting the words between her teeth. "*At least you don't have to howl about it.*"

Someone opened the door and Jill turned to see Sally. Sally had just heard the news. She was loyally indignant. "It's just a shame, Jilly. Old Bailey's a crab. Everybody says it wasn't fair of her to put Kathy in your place. Gosh, I was so worried when I couldn't find you."

"You needn't have been. I'm O.K." Jill met Sally's eyes in the mirror as she leaned forward to put a last dab of powder on her nose. "And it wasn't Miss Bailey's fault. Or Kathy's, either. It was mine, I guess. Anyway"—Jill drew a long breath and managed to smile—"it's over. Remember what Chuck used to say: 'That's the way the cookie crumbles.'"

"That's the way the mop flops," Sally finished.

"Let's forget it," Jill said. "We'll have to race if we want to catch the bus."

But forgetting wasn't easy. Not even for Jill, who could usually forget so quickly. Riding home on the bus, she could still feel the hot waves of anger—and still she wasn't quite sure who she was angry at. Not Miss Bailey; certainly not Kathy. And not Alex, really. If only she hadn't flared back at him. . . . Somehow that memory made her feel the worst of all. Maybe she was most angry at herself.

That evening Jill told the news at home. Her father only said, "That's too bad, Jill. I'm sorry."

Jo Ann sputtered furiously. "It just wasn't fair. Everybody at school says Miss Bailey's an old meanie."

Jill's mother said very little. But after Jill's light was out that night, her mother came and sat on the edge of the bed. She put her arms around Jill. "It's a hard lesson, I know," she said. "But, honey, it's a lesson you're just going to have to learn some time. You can't go on spoiling your chances at everything. You just can't have things without working for them."

When the door was closed and she was alone, Jill flopped over on the pillow. It was all right with Mommy and Daddy, she thought. They were disappointed, but they always understood. But she wished again there were some way she could tell Alex she was sorry.

The more Jill remembered the way Alex had looked, the more she realized that he had given her the first real chance to be friends.

She wondered if he would ever give her another chance.

The next week was the fall picnic. All the Merrymakers, even Jill, forgot their troubles.

"It's our last chance for a cookout before the weather turns cold," Mr. Miller said. "I understand the He-Man Chefs Club is serving the refreshments and I understand they are going to be *something*."

Sally's brother, Jerry, was one of the He-Man Chefs. "You better be careful what you eat," Sally warned Jill. "I've heard Jerry talking to some of his friends on the telephone about the concoctions they're planning to serve. I think we'd better take peanut-butter sandwiches with us, just to be on the safe side."

The He-Man Chefs had spent eight weeks learning to cook perfectly sensible things like scrambled eggs and bacon, baked beans, corn muffins, and cherry pie. The high point of the course was when they learned to make pizza. And for the picnic they produced trays and trays of pizza, piping hot. Pizza plain, pizza with sausage, pizza with bacon and olives.

"We needn't have worried about the food," Sally said to Jill. "It's delicious!"

The guests ate until they were stuffed.

Then came the big event of the evening—the free-style Dagwood sandwich contest.

Each He-Man Chef had a stack of bread. Every sort of filling was set out on a platter.

The contest was to see which He-Man could make the biggest sandwich with the weirdest assortment of things in it. The test was that each He-Man had to be able to eat his own production.

Jill and Sally sat on the side lines with the other girls, marveling and groaning as the boys piled up the layers. Peanut butter on tomato on bologna, on jelly on ham on cheese, on honey on pickle. . . .

The stacks of horrible mixtures grew higher and higher. But the boys bit in and swallowed bravely.

The judges named Tim Stanford the winner and Mr. Miller presented the prize. Tim staggered up to take it and burst out laughing.

The prize was a package of *Tums*.

After the picnic there was a hayride under the stars. Jill lay back, looking up at the bright-spangled sky. She wished she could read her fortune in the stars. She wondered if they held good luck for her. . . .

CHAPTER 7

One More Chance

On Thanksgiving evening the first snow fell.

It was just enough to frost the fields and make a thin, slippery coating on the roads. Headlights of cars on the highway shone like big hazy globes through the white mist.

Jill's father was driving the family home, in the early dusk, from a dinner at Grandmother Miller's house in Dale Valley.

"Oh, dear," Mrs. Miller sighed, "I was bound and determined not to eat too much this year, but I never can resist Grandmother's cooking. It was delicious. Only I hope I don't *hear* of another turkey before Christmas!"

"*Gobble, gobble.* I'm a turkey," Jo Ann murmured drowsily. She was curled up on the back seat, her head on Jill's shoulder.

Jill was half asleep herself. She was full of good dinner. The night before they had come home late from a square-dance party the County 4-H Council had given in honor of their leaders. Jill was too sleepy to listen to another word. She gave a last yawn and settled her head comfortably on top of Jo-Jo's pigtails. She was just drifting off to sleep when something her father said brought her suddenly wide-awake.

Mr. Miller was talking about Alex. "I've asked the boy to

come over to the ranch Saturday," he said. "I want him to look at Dolly. I don't like the way the mare has been acting, and when Dr. Young saw her last week he wasn't encouraging. Doc says she has the heaves pretty badly. And being in foal has made her worse. I may have to send her away, but I want Alex's opinion first. I've never seen a boy understand animals the way he does. Ed Marshall says he almost seems to talk to them."

"He's done wonders with Laddie," Jill's mother said.

Mr. Miller nodded. "It's remarkable," he said. "He's training the horse to good riding manners, and he's almost cured Lad's lame leg—goodness only knows how. When I asked Alex how he did it, he said he rubbed the leg some, and talked to the horse a little—just sort of made him feel easy." Mr. Miller shook his head and laughed. "It sounds more like old-fashioned home remedies than veterinary science, but it seems to work. I don't know whether he can help Dolly or not, but I don't intend to send her away until Alex has seen her."

Jill was sitting up straight in the back seat, listening. If Alex was coming to the ranch on Saturday, she'd have to see him, of course. Jill hadn't admitted to herself until that very minute how she had been avoiding Alex ever since the day at school when she had lost her part in the play. In math class she had tried to find a seat as far away from him as she could. At school games or in the lunchroom, she had been careful not to sit near him. Even at the 4-H party the night before, she had somehow managed to keep out of Alex's way. But if Daddy had asked him to the ranch tomorrow, how could she possibly not come face-to-face with him?

One thing anyway, Jill decided. She wouldn't be silly and

try to run away. If Alex was still angry with her, she'd just have to take it.

The next evening *Our Town* was given at the school.

Jill sat in the audience with Sally. She watched Kathy Donaldson play the part of Emily.

It made Jill feel queer to hear Kathy say the lines she might have been saying herself.

The performance was so good Jill soon forgot everything and just enjoyed it. When it was over, she said to Sally, "Kathy was wonderful." She truly meant it, yet she couldn't help a last twinge of regret.

Miss Bailey had said Jill would have chances for parts in other plays, but there would never be another chance of playing Emily.

When Alex came to the Miller ranch on Saturday, he showed no sign of being angry. He spoke to Jill quite matter-of-factly. Then he and Mr. Miller got straight to business. They walked out to the barn, talking earnestly.

When Jill followed, keeping a little distance behind, neither her father nor Alex seemed to notice her.

Standing by herself, Jill watched Alex look over the little mare. She saw him put his hands on Dolly's side and then bend down and put his ear close while he listened to her heavy, painful breathing,

There was no doubt about it, Alex told Mr. Miller, the mare had the heaves. And she was bound to get worse before her foal was born. "Unless she has special feeding and handling and careful exercise, I'm afraid you can't hope to pull her through." Alex shook his head. "It's too bad. A mare with a tendency to heaves shouldn't have been bred in the first place."

"I know," Mr. Miller said. "That's just what Dr. Young said. I suppose I was foolish to have picked up a mare that had already been bred without knowing more about her. But she's always been a pet and I hated to see her sold to a dealer. Now the question is, what can we do? All this special feeding and handling the mare needs will take time, and that's one thing I haven't got. With the rest of my stock and the ranch to manage, I have more work than I can do as it is."

"I wish I could help you," Alex said. He patted Dolly's neck. The mare stood very still under Alex's hand, almost as if she knew something important were being decided.

"She's a nice little horse," Alex went on, "but I couldn't ask Uncle Ed to let me keep her for you. His barn is crowded now. I had to fix up an extra stall myself to make a place for Laddie. There's just no room to bring another horse in."

Mr. Miller shook his head. "I wouldn't think of expecting it," he said. "I am afraid I'll have to let Dolly go. Dr. Young says they might take her at Smith's ranch over in the next county if I'd be willing to give them the foal."

Alex looked up with a quick frown. "What sort of care will she get there?" he asked.

"Oh, the best, Doc says. Smith's is a breeding farm—the biggest in this part of the state."

"Too big, maybe." Alex's frown deepened. "Especially for a mare like this one. Dolly's used to being a pet. She won't think much of being just a—number."

"I know she won't get the kind of attention we'd give her," Mr. Miller admitted, "but there's just no choice. Well"—he started to turn away—"thanks anyway. I wanted your opinion before I told Doc to go ahead with the arrangements."

Until that moment Jill had stood perfectly still. Now, suddenly, almost before she realized what she was going to say, she was beside her father. "Let me take care of Dolly," she asked her father. "I can do it, Daddy. I know I can. If Alex will tell me what to do and show me how to do it, I can do every single thing Dolly needs and you won't have to send her away. Please, Daddy—"

Jill stopped as her father shook his head. She saw the look of doubt that came over Alex's face. "Oh, I know, I know," she hurried on. "You think I won't keep my word. I don't blame you for thinking it, when I've failed so often. But this time I *will* keep it—if you'll trust me just once more."

Mr. Miller still hesitated. "Now, wait a minute, Jilly, not so fast," he said. "It's not a question of trusting you. But taking care of this mare is going to be a mighty hard job. Remember, she won't foal for another two months. Even then, if she comes through safely, she'll still need plenty of care; so will her colt. I just don't want you to take on something that will be too much for you."

"It wouldn't be too much." Jill shook her head. "I know I can do it. Look at all the time I waste on movies and TV and talking to Sally on the telephone. I'll give up every one of them and spend every minute working with Dolly." As her father still looked doubtful, Jill took a last desperate plunge. "Daddy," she said, "if Alex says I can do it, then will you let me?"

Before her father could answer, Jill swung around to face Alex squarely. "Alex," she said, "I'm sorry I said what I did the day you called me dumb. I *was* dumb to lose that part in the play, and I hadn't any right to be mad at you for saying it. But I don't want to be dumb all my life. I want to start changing—if you'll just help me. Will you, Alex?" Jill was really pleading. "Please, Alex?"

For a minute that seemed endless to Jill, Alex looked straight at her. His face never moved a flicker. The mask that had come over it the day in the hall at school was still there, unchanged. He took a slow breath. Jill's heart sank.

Surely he was going to say "no."

At that moment the mare moved. She put her head against the boy's shoulder. Alex turned toward her for a moment. Dolly's soft brown glance was trusting. "Please help me," Dolly seemed to be saying. "Please trust her."

Alex looked back at Jill.

"All right," Alex said. He spoke evenly, not smiling. "If you'll take care of Dolly, and your father is willing to let you, I'll help as much as I can."

"Alex was going to say 'no'—I'm sure he was," Jill told Sally later. "It was Dolly who changed his mind."

Next morning Alex was back. Jill was ready and waiting. She was wearing blue jeans and Chuck's old gray sweater. For the next hour she listened while Alex told her how to take care of Dolly. She was determined not to miss a single word or forget one thing he said.

First of all, Alex explained, she had to understand that heaves in a horse was like an allergy in a person. Any kind of dust made a horse heave more. And one really bad heaving spell could kill a mare in Dolly's condition.

Hay and grain were full of dust. So the first thing was to wet down Dolly's feed. Her grain must be made into a mash mixed with water—one measure in the morning, vitamins mixed in; the second part in the evening. Even her hay had to be wet. "You have to soak it overnight," Alex said. "One night in vinegar and water, the next night in lime water; and give it to her wet the next day. You can't soak it too long or it spoils." But if either the grain or the hay were dry, she'd breathe dust when she ate it, and that might start her heaving.

For exercise, Alex went on, the mare needed at least an hour every day. She couldn't be ridden and she couldn't be turned loose in pasture. "It means walking her," Alex said. "Lead her carefully, but keep her moving. Take her outdoors if the weather is good. In the barn if it's raining. But an hour or more every day. Do you understand?"

Jill nodded. She had understood everything. Alex explained things carefully and showed her exactly what to do, quietly, patiently. There was still no sign of the moment's friendliness she had seen the one day at school. Jill once more wondered if she would ever see his face without the guarded look again. But that didn't matter now.

She'd given her promise and she would show Daddy and Alex she meant to keep it.

That evening, after Jill had bedded Dolly for the night, Jill stood in the stall and listened to the mare's breathing. Maybe she was imagining, but already it sounded a little easier. She laid her forehead against the warm neck.

"You gave me one more chance, Dolly," she whispered. "I won't fail this time."

CHAPTER 8

4-H Saddle Club

The days flew by so quickly that Jill was suddenly startled to find Christmas only a week away. "I can't understand it," she told her mother. "When I was little, I used to think it was so long between Thanksgiving and Christmas I couldn't bear to wait. Now there isn't half enough time. It simply races." She sighed. "I guess I must be growing old," she added sadly.

Her mother didn't laugh. She stopped by the kitchen table, where Jill sat, and gave Jill's blond pony tail a light pat. "I don't see very many gray hairs yet," she teased gently. "Maybe you're not growing old, just growing up."

"Well, I feel a million years old." Jill put her head down on her arms. "It seems to me I've been sleepy ever since I can remember."

Her mother looked down sympathetically, but she said nothing. She knew what a struggle it had been for Jill to get up an hour earlier every morning to get out to the barn and take care of Dolly. But she knew it was a struggle Jill would have to win or lose by herself.

The first few mornings, when the alarm had rung, Jill had longed to reach over and strangle it and then go back to sleep. But she was determined. Somehow she had made herself get up. Part of her determination was to show Daddy, and part of her determination was to show Alex she had really meant it when she promised to take care of the little mare.

Every few days Alex came by. He looked Dolly over carefully each time. Jill kept hoping Alex would say something to show that he realized how hard she was working. Yet no matter how she knocked herself out to follow every detail of his directions about taking care of Dolly, Alex never gave her a word of praise. He only nodded when he found Dolly all right, or made a suggestion when he thought the mare needed some extra care.

"I guess there's no use hoping for compliments from Alex," Jill told Sally with a sigh. "It's funny, though," she added thoughtfully, "I really started working with Dolly just to prove I could take on a job and finish it. I wasn't thinking half as much about helping Dolly as I was about showing Alex and Daddy I could do it. But now that I've worked with Dolly, and watched her get a little better every day"—Jill paused—"it's *Dolly* I care about. I guess I wouldn't give her up whether anyone else knew what I was doing or not."

Nevertheless, Jill's cheeks flushed with pleasure on the day when Alex, leaning over Dolly's hoof, said quite casually, "Oh, by the way, Jerry and I have that 4-H horse project pretty well organized now. Nancy Barnes even has a fancy name for it. She wants to call it the Merrymakers Saddle Club. Nancy has borrowed a Tennessee walking horse from her cousin, and Deedee Lane's taken over an old wagon horse someone wanted to give away. You should see how she's spruced the poor old critter up! Tim Stanford and Gig Williamson are asking Scotty to help them get mares from the Saddle Horse Association. The association lets 4-H members borrow a mare in foal. Then the member gets to keep the colt. If you wanted to join"—Alex was bending down, listening to Dolly's breathing as he spoke—"you could have Dolly as a project. I told Scotty you were getting along O.K. He said he'd bring you a project book if you want to start keeping the record."

Jill felt the glow warm her cheeks. It wasn't exactly extravagant praise from Alex. Still, it was the first real friendliness he had shown since the day in the hall at school. She wanted to thank him somehow for all the patient help he had given her with Dolly; but before she could manage a word, he had interrupted with an explanation about how a horse's feet should be checked every day to be sure no stones were wedged between the shoe and the hoof.

The next meeting of the Saddle Club was at Tim Stanford's house and Jill was welcomed as a new member. Scotty had given Jill a project book that afternoon and showed her how she must enter every detail, with dates and costs, showing her care of Dolly, and Dolly's foal after it was born. "Good luck on your project," Scotty had said. "Alex is one of the best junior leaders I've ever had, but he'll make you work hard!"

Jill had only nodded. She already knew that.

Still, she was glad Alex had asked her to be in the Saddle Club. At the meeting, when the others talked rather bewilderingly about gaits and martingales and conformation, Jill was pleased that she at least understood what the terms meant.

She had hoped that Alex might seem less serious and

impersonal in the club, but she was disappointed. "You just can't expect Alex to be friendly," Nancy Barnes confided to Jill. "He's wonderful about helping us with our work, but he just doesn't think there's any use talking to people—except about horses."

One day Alex brought the Saddle Club members to the Miller ranch. He and Jill took them out to the barn to see Dolly. They explained to the other members how they were trying to help the little mare by giving her special care until her foal was born.

Jill had Dolly's coat brushed smoothly, and a ribbon braided in her mane in honor of the visitors.

Scotty had driven over with the club members. Afterward he stayed to have dinner with the Millers.

When Scotty had left, Mr. Miller asked Jill an odd question. "Jill," he said, "did Alex ever tell you that he had owned a horse named Charger?"

Jill glanced up, startled. "Yes, once."

"What did he say about it?" Her father looked unusually serious.

"Well, just that he had it—" Jill hesitated. She was remembering the day when Alex had suddenly stopped speaking, and she saw his fists doubled tightly. Somehow she didn't feel that she should tell her father about it—any more than she had felt she should tell Sally. "Alex didn't say any more," she finished.

Mr. Miller was silent for a moment. Then he said, "It's a peculiar thing—Scotty says Alex has talked a good deal about his horse Charger. But when Scotty mentioned it to Ed Marshall, Ed said he didn't believe Alex has ever had a horse of his own. Of course, Alex and his family lived a long way from here, and Ed might not have known that Alex had a horse. In any case, Scotty says Alex seems to have thought a great deal of this horse Charger."

"I'm sure he did." Jill nodded. She was thinking again of Alex's tight fists.

CHAPTER 9

Wishbone

After the next Saddle Club meeting, Alex drove Jill home, and something happened that made Jill puzzle more than ever about Alex.

On the way back Jill pointed suddenly to a small figure beside the road. "Look, Alex," she exclaimed. "That's a puppy! What in the world would it be doing out here so far from any house?"

Alex stopped the car. They both got out, and the next minute they were bending over a forlorn little creature. The puppy was brown and white. Its coat was matted with mud; it was so thin that every spindly rib stood out, and a wispy tail quivered between its hind legs.

"Oh, poor little thing," Jill breathed. "It must have wandered away from home. Maybe we can take it back, if we can find out who lost it—"

"Nobody lost it."

Alex's words cut Jill short. She looked up and was amazed to see his gray eyes blazing. "Nobody lost it," he said again. His voice was bitter with anger. "Somebody left the puppy here on purpose, to get rid of it."

"Oh, but they wouldn't, Alex," Jill protested. "Who would do anything so mean?"

"Plenty of people." Alex's mouth settled in a grim line. "There isn't anything so mean that people won't do it."

Jill felt herself stiffen with indignation. "That's not fair," she said. "You can't possibly know that anyone meant to get rid of the puppy. Why do you always think people are wrong and mean, and only animals aren't?"

When Alex made no answer for a moment, Jill was sorry her words had burst out before she thought. She remembered the other time she had flared back at Alex, and how long it had been before he was even halfway friendly again. "I'm sorry, Alex," she began. "I didn't mean to—"

He didn't give her a chance to finish. "You asked a question," he said. "I'll answer it. *I don't trust people because they always let you down. Animals never do.*"

The strange bitterness was still in Alex's voice. Yet somehow Jill knew that this time his anger was not meant for her. It was for something else—something that must have happened long ago to make him hate people. There was no way of guessing what it could have been.

Jill wished there were some way to tell Alex he was wrong —that no matter what had happened, people weren't all bad, any more than they were all good. She started to speak, but just then she looked down and saw Alex's hands.

His fists were doubled as she had seen them once before— the day he had spoken of Charger—clenched so tightly that the knuckles showed white.

The words Jill had been going to speak died in her throat. Something about the tenseness in Alex's hands stopped her, just as it had stopped her the other time.

"Anyway," Jill said after a moment, quietly, "whatever happened isn't the puppy's fault. We can take him home and try to help him. I don't think Mommy will mind much.

Since our collie died we haven't any dog except Cindy, and she's old."

Jill reached down to pick up the little dog; but Alex's hands, the fists unclenched now, lifted him first. She saw how gently Alex gathered up the thin little body.

The little dog rode back to the ranch on the seat between them. Frightened as he was, he seemed, little by little, to understand that he could trust them. When Jill reached down to pat him, he even put out a timid, pink tongue and licked her hand.

Mrs. Miller took the stray puppy's arrival good-naturedly. Long years of experience with Chuck, who had, in his time, brought home everything from a pigeon with a broken wing to a sackful of kittens he had saved from drowning, had made Mrs. Miller philosophical about strange arrivals in the family.

"The first thing is to get some food into him," Mrs. Miller said. "We'd better start with a little warm milk and then work up to something more substantial."

Jill brought out a saucer. A few minutes later they were watching the hungry guest lap milk so eagerly that he finished with a ring of white around his little muzzle. By the time he had emptied a second dish of meat and cereal, they could actually see his tummy bulge.

"Go find Cindy's old basket for him to sleep in," Jill's mother said.

When Jill and Alex went out to the barn to look for the basket, the puppy waddled behind them companionably. But they had reckoned without Cindy, who did not share Mrs. Miller's philosophical attitude toward strangers in her domain. Cindy was too polite to bite. She simply glared at the puppy, uttered a few huffy growls, and then retired to her own bed and settled herself with a bone between her paws. The puppy stared, keeping a respectful distance, but the expression in his eyes was so full of envy as he watched the big dog gnaw on the delicious-looking bone that Jill burst out laughing.

"Did you ever see anything funnier?" she said. "The puppy just wishing for that bone." She turned to Alex with a sudden idea. "What a perfect name for the puppy— Wishbone!"

That night Wishbone slept in his basket in the cellar. Jill and Jo Ann watched him settle down with a sigh of pure contentment and a last wag of his wispy tail.

"I guess his tail is about run down," Jo Ann said. "He's wagged it every minute since he got here."

They gave him a good-night pat and Wishbone's brown eyes looked up lovingly.

Going upstairs, Jill thought again of Alex's puzzling words that afternoon. She wondered what had happened to make Alex so sure he couldn't trust people. Whatever the reason was, he was locking it up inside himself—the same way he tightened his clenched fists.

Jill sighed. If only it were as easy to make a *person* trust people as it had been to teach the frightened little puppy to trust them, Jill thought, how much nicer the world would be.

On the last weekend before Christmas vacation Jill came home from school feeling miserable. Her throat was scratchy and her head ached.

She longed to go straight upstairs to bed. Instead, she changed into her old clothes and went out to the barn to take care of Dolly.

Even with Chuck's gray sweater on, and an extra scarf tied over her head, Jill shivered with cold as she measured Dolly's grain, mixed the mash with hot water, and put the special wet hay into Dolly's bin. After that was done, Jill still had to give the mare her exercise. Leading Dolly patiently back and forth, back and forth, Jill looked at her watch a dozen times, wondering if the hour would ever end. Her legs and back ached with weariness.

When at last Dolly was settled for the night, Jill came in the house. Her mother was putting supper on the table, but Jill didn't even glance at the lamb stew and dumplings.

She went straight upstairs and climbed into bed. In an instant she was sound asleep.

It seemed like hours later when Jill woke to see her father standing beside her with a tray. He had brought her hot broth and toast. Jill blinked in astonishment. When she was sick it was always Mommy who brought trays. But Daddy put the tray carefully down on her knees. "I'll be back when you finish," he said.

Jill took a sip of hot soup and felt it comfort her raw throat. She was hungrier than she realized. She finished the last bite of toast and jelly and licked her fingers, then she sat back against the pillow with a comfortable sigh.

Maybe she wasn't going to be really sick after all.

"I'll be all right in the morning," Jill told her father when he came back. But he stopped a moment by the bed.

"No, you rest tomorrow, Jilly," he said. "I'll take care of Dolly for you."

It was all he said, but it was enough. Jill settled back. She drifted off to sleep again, smiling drowsily to herself. If Daddy had used all the words in the dictionary, he couldn't have told her any more plainly that he was pleased with her. She snuggled deliciously into the pillow. Her headache was almost gone. How wonderful to think she could sleep as long as she liked in the morning! No alarm clock set, no chores to get up for.

Bless Daddy, she thought gratefully. Bless daddies and mothers and *people*.

Alex was a dope not to believe that people could be as nice as animals.

CHAPTER 10

Christmas Is Everywhere

When Jill awoke the next morning she was amazed to see the sun high in the sky outside her window. It took her a moment to remember that she had special permission to sleep late. Then she stretched and yawned. Finally she got up to put on her quilted housecoat and the fur-lined slippers Jo-Jo had given her last Christmas.

Padding downstairs, Jill found the breakfast table already cleared and the kitchen empty. She looked in the living room and saw Jo Ann standing on a chair, polishing the mirror above the mantel. Cleaning the downstairs rooms was the girls' regular Saturday morning chore.

"Hi." Jo Ann looked at Jill. "We wondered if you were still alive. Mom's outside, cleaning chickens to put in the freezer. She said you could make some tea and toast for breakfast if you felt better. Do you?"

"I guess I'm all well." Jill nodded. She sounded a little surprised. She saw the vacuum cleaner that Jo Ann had brought out, ready to use, and her conscience pricked her. Vacuuming was usually Jill's task. "I feel fine really. Just leave the vacuum, Jo-Jo. I'll finish the room later."

"Gee, thanks." Jo Ann hopped down from the chair quickly. "I told Dot I'd come over if I could. We're trying to figure out what kind of blouses and skirts to make for our sewing project." She whisked up her dustcloth and polish, and hurried to get her jacket.

Jill went back to the kitchen. It was usually a busy room. It was strange and rather nice to find it so empty and quiet. She put the kettle on to boil, dropped a slice of bread into the toaster, and walked over to look at Mom's row of geraniums on the window sill. After her third slice of toast, the last two with honey, and a bowl of cereal, Jill was sure she was quite recovered.

She cleared the table and wandered back to the living room. She needn't hurry about the vacuuming. She might as well enjoy her morning of leisure.

Looking for something to do, Jill crossed to the small room her father used for an office, where he kept the ranch accounts. Jill sat down in front of the typewriter. Just for fun she slipped in a sheet of paper and sat staring at it. If she couldn't be an actress, maybe she could write stories and be a famous author. If only she could think of a plot!

Suddenly a brilliant idea struck her. Why not start a newspaper for the 4-H Saddle Club? She could write up notes and jokes, and make carbon copies to give the members. The others could help her get news. She thought a moment more, and then typed out the title in careful capitals: THE HOOFPRINT.

She went on, typing faster and faster, chuckling to herself as she thought of item after item. She barely glanced up when her mother came in to ask how she felt.

"Fine," she murmured absently. "Just fine." She was frowning over the keyboard, trying to remember whether *embarrass* had two "r's" or just one.

Even when she went in to finish tidying up the living

room as she had promised Jo-Jo she would, Jill's mind was still on her writing. She ran the vacuum energetically, poking its noisy nose under chairs and tables and into corners, mumbling new paragraphs to herself.

The Pattersons stopped by after lunch and Jill could scarcely wait to show Jerry the *Hoofprint* copy.

"Hey, this isn't bad," Jerry said. "I have a couple of ideas myself. There ought to be something about that shed Alex and Tim have been trying to build." Jerry sat down at the typewriter and began to peck the keys with two fingers.

"And we could have a casualty column," Jill said. "Just think how often we fall off."

The two went on working together. By late afternoon they had the first edition ready, with carbon copies.

At the next meeting, the other members of the Saddle Club were delighted with the *Hoofprint*. They read it, laughing, and began suggesting news items and jokes for the next issue.

The only one who didn't join in the general enthusiasm was Alex. Jill was sitting with Nancy Barnes when they saw Alex take up a copy of the *Hoofprint*. He only glanced at it, not smiling. Then he waited for the others to finish reading before he called the meeting to order.

"For goodness sake," Nancy whispered indignantly to Jill, "I wish Alex would relax just once, and let us have a little fun!"

Johnny Lane and Chuck came home from the University for vacation the day before Christmas Eve. They drove up to the Miller ranch in Chuck's old jalopy, and came into the house to find Sally and Carol, with Jill and Jo Ann, surrounded by yards of red and green ribbon and paper

THE HOOF ∩ PRINT

irregular, irresistible chronicle of the

Merrymakers Saddle Club

Editor-in-Chief: Jill Miller
Staff: anyone who feels energetic enough to contribute

OUR NEW DOCTOR

Newest friend and member of the SADDLE CLUB is Dr. William Young, who has consented to become our veterinarian and adviser. Dr. Young, better known as "Doc," comes to meetings, listens to our troubles, and gives advice on everything from spavins to Tim's problems in attracting the attention of a certain curly-haired owner of a palomino colt. "Doc" has always been interested in horses, and he rides saddle seat.
He is very good-natured and is rarely in a bad mood. The only thing that puts him in a bad mood is dumb women.

Names of our latest
Stable Animals:
Scoobie: three-color kitten
Henrietta: chicken
Joe: black dog
Cleopatra: cat
Rats: too many to mention!

IS your horse falling down?
DOES he, or she, need support?

Place your ad in this paper.

LOST a horseshoe?
FIND it in the YELLOW PAGES.
(adv.)

NANCY'S SWEET SIXTEEN PARTY SUCCESS

The sweet-sixteen party given for and by Nancy Kelly turned out successfully. Everybody attended except those who absolutely couldn't.

NOTE TO MEMBERS:

PLEASE BRING FOOD FOR STABLE CATS -- OR ELSE GET SMALLER RATS. . . .

NEWS:

On the occasion of our last 4-H Saddle Club moonlight ride, Sunny, popular, vitamin-packed saddle horse, became indignant because he had no rider, and broke loose from his stall to join the party. His efforts were in vain. He was escorted back to the barn.

REMINDER:

Advertisements make the newspaper thicker.

CASUALTY COLUMN STARTS
NEXT WEEK. . .

SOCIAL NOTE:

On St. Patrick's Day there will be a Saddle Club Party to celebrate St. Patrick's Day.

BUY AT FORCE FEEDS FOR SLOW AND SURE DELIVERY.
Our motto: "We'll be prompt, no matter how long it takes."
(adv.)

UNSTABLE STABLE

During the past three weeks Alex, Tim, and Jerry have been trying to put together an un-cooperative shed to house two new colts on the Patterson farm. The question has arisen as to what will happen when the first playful zephyr comes along and no one is there to hold onto the shed except the colts.

THINGS THAT MAKE A BAD IMPRESSION:

Singing love songs in the presence of one's parents.

FALL OFF YOUR HORSE
AND GET IN THE PAPER!

wrapping. They were getting the last gift packages ready for the Merrymakers to take to patients in the Dale Valley Hospital.

Everyone rushed to greet Johnny and Chuck. "You're just in time," Jill said. "We're going to sing carols at the hospital tonight and we're terribly short of basses. Scotty is coming, but he just growls. And neither Tim nor Gig can carry a tune."

"You're saved," Johnny said. "The original Kansas Kanaries have arrived. But you'll have to feed us first. Chuck's chariot had more flat tires than usual on the way home, and we ran out of money. So all we've had to eat since lunch were a couple of hamburgers and chocolate malteds. In other words, we're starving!"

When Mrs. Miller brought out a chocolate cake, the boys' faces lighted. Carol poured coffee, and Jill saw the way Carol's eyes shone as she looked at Johnny.

That night, at the hospital, Jill watched Carol again.

First the Merrymakers went through each corridor, carrying lighted candles and singing carols. Then they visited the wards, bringing their packages and stopping to talk to the patients.

Jill saw Carol stop for a word with each sick person. Carol's touch was gentle and sure, as she straightened a cover or smoothed a pillow.

No wonder Carol wants to be a nurse, Jill thought. She saw the patients' eyes follow Carol as long as she was in sight. In a dress of warm gold wool, the same color as her hair, with a sprig of dark-green holly and crimson berries on her shoulder, Carol looked like the very spirit of Christmas.

Following Carol, Jill was surprised to find how easy it

was to find a word to say, and how quickly the patients' smiles met her own.

At the end of one corridor there was a room with a closed door.

"I don't know that you'd better go in there," one of the nurses whispered warningly. "Mrs. D. is one of our difficult patients. She's been here longer than anyone else on the floor, and she doesn't encourage visitors. To tell you the truth"—the nurse shrugged—"we're all afraid of her."

Carol and Jill looked at each other. "I dare if you dare," Carol said.

Jill nodded. She and Carol went in the room together. "She can't do any worse than bite our heads off," Jill whispered.

Jill had expected someone fierce and frowny. She stopped short in surprise as they saw, instead, a tiny woman with bright-blue eyes and neatly curled white hair sitting stiffly against the pillows. She might have been quite pretty except for the sharp lines that dragged her mouth down at the corners.

"Merry Christmas," Carol said, and walked toward the bed.

The woman's sharp blue eyes looked back. "It doesn't seem very merry to me," she snapped.

Jill would have given up and fled, but Carol went on, talking so easily and pleasantly that, in spite of herself, the woman's tight mouth relaxed. She even smiled a little.

Just as they left, the old lady took Carol's hand. "I never thought I'd believe in Christmas again," she said, "but seeing you makes me remember old times—long ago."

When they said good-by there was actually a twinkle in the old lady's eye. "You girls might come and see me again,"

68

she said. "That is, if you dare. Most of the nurses are afraid to come near me for fear I'll bite."

"How was she?" the nurse asked, as the girls closed the door behind them. "Did she roar at you?"

Jill and Carol laughed.

"Only a little roar," Carol said. "In fact, she seemed quite tame before we left. Maybe she doesn't mean to be difficult. Maybe she's just lonely. Anyway, we promised to come and see her again. And we will."

"I wish you luck," the nurse said. "If you can improve Mrs. D.'s disposition, everyone in the hospital will thank you!"

Christmas Eve was always fun in the Miller house. They hung their stockings, wrapped last-minute presents, and whispered secrets to each other about tomorrow's surprises.

The Pattersons stopped by after supper. Sally was bursting with excitement. "Guess what I'm getting for Christmas?" she asked Jill. "Twin calves! They were born last night and Daddy says they're mine. They're even cuter than Hotty and Fatty were when they were born. I named one Pete, but the other one's such a funny little pet, I can't call him anything but Cuddles. Jerry thinks that's a terrible name for a calf, but I don't care."

Carol and Johnny came in later. They had a wonderful surprise, too. "Johnny had a letter from medical school," Carol said. "He's been accepted for next year. He'll start studying in the fall to be a doctor."

Carol herself would be leaving to start her nurse's training at the same time.

After they had gone Mrs. Miller said thoughtfully, "I wonder if Johnny will really be able to finish his medical

69

training. It takes so many years to study to be a doctor, I just hope his family can manage it."

"He'll manage," Jill's father said. "Johnny has dreamed of being a doctor ever since he was a little boy bandaging a puppy's hurt paw. Anyone who wants a thing as much as Johnny wants to be a doctor, will find a way to get it."

"And he's lucky to have Carol to help him." Mrs. Miller nodded. "If ever two young people were born for each other, it's Carol and Johnny."

Next morning, after church, Jill went to the Pattersons' to see Sally's new calves. The two girls hovered over the stall, looking at the newborn babies. Pete was standing on his wobbly legs with his furry coat freshly licked and his flat little white face turned toward them. Cuddles, true to his name, lay snuggled next to his mother.

"They're simply beautiful," Jill said, "but just wait until Dolly's foal is born. Then *I'll* have something to be proud of."

Walking toward the door, past the long row of stalls, Jill saw the winter sunlight stream through the high windows, across the stacks of golden hay. There was no sound except the quiet breathing of the animals and the soft rustling as they moved in their stalls.

The wonderful thing about Christmas was that it could be everywhere at once, Jill thought. It was at home, and in the lighted candles in the church. It was in the hospital, and in the school program. It was here in the gentle peacefulness of the barn.

CHAPTER 11

Dawn's Wonder

It was a stormy night in January when Jill knew that Dolly's foal was going to be born.

For the last week Jill had been worried. In spite of all their care, Dolly's breathing had become painfully hard. Alex had come by almost every day. But there was nothing he could do. He and Jill could only stand beside the stall, watching the little mare heave for each breath.

"Is she going to be all right?" Jill asked Alex, over and over.

"I hope so," was all Alex would say. But Jill always felt better when Alex stood beside her. In spite of his silence, Jill was sure that Alex knew how she was suffering for the brave little mare. "After all Dolly and I have been through together. I just can't let anything happen to her," Jill said desperately. "It's so awful to know that she needs help, and not to be able to give it to her."

The rest of the Miller family had watched over Dolly as anxiously as Jill. Chuck even wrote from college: "How are the mothers-to-be, Dolly and Jill?"

"Dr. Young has promised to come over when Dolly foals," Jill's father had said. "He knows she's going to have a hard time."

But when the night came, a sleeting rain was falling, and the freezing wind turned the roads to a glare of ice.

Jill came in from the barn, her blue eyes filled with distress. "I just know it's going to happen tonight," she said. "Dolly's walking back and forth and back and forth in her stall. And, Daddy, her breathing is awful. She's just gasping! Can we get Dr. Young?"

"I'm afraid Doc can't possibly make it on a night like this —or Alex, either." Mr. Miller shook his head soberly. "If Dolly foals tonight, we'll have to manage alone, the best we can."

Later, when Jill and her father stood beside the stall, Jill's hands were clasped. With every gasping breath that Dolly drew, Jill could feel the pain herself. "I never knew I could care about anything as much as this," she said finally, in a low voice.

"I know it's hard, Jilly." Mr. Miller nodded soberly. He looked anxiously at Jill's white face. "Maybe you'd better go back to the house and wait."

Jill turned. For a moment she was willing to go. Then the barn door opened and Alex came through, stamping his wet boots. The roads were too slippery to drive. Alex had walked the two miles. Jill breathed again. *Alex is here,* she thought. *Alex can help Dolly if anyone can.*

Alex went straight to Dolly. He bent down and touched her gently. He talked to her, trying to give her strength. The little mare struggled on bravely. But her long, harsh breaths were coming more slowly.

Alex looked up. "We can't save her," he said to Mr. Miller. "She's heaving too badly. There are some drugs that might help. But unless Dr. Young gets here in time, I'm afraid she won't make it."

Jill closed her eyes. "Alex can't help," she told herself. She heard the icy wind howl outside the barn. "And Dr. Young can't possibly get here. Oh, Dolly," she begged silently, "don't give up. Please try, just a little longer."

When the barn door was flung open, they turned in astonishment. Dr. Young couldn't have made it, but there he was —his black bag in his hand, his cap and collar frosted with ice.

"Now, let's see what we can do," he said. He had his coat off and was rolling up his sleeves. After one quick look at Dolly, he opened his bag. "I'll try an injection of cortisone," he said. "That should help her breathe. If she can just breathe, she'll have a chance."

Jill saw the needle plunge into Dolly's flank. She closed her eyes again.

Then, slowly, incredibly, Jill heard the mare's hard, rasping breaths grow easier. She kept her eyes shut, not daring to look until she heard the doctor's voice again.

"Dolly's made it!" Dr. Young said. "Good girl, Dolly. That was a real fight."

Slowly, Jill opened her eyes. A wave of thankfulness swept over her.

"You've got a colt, Jill," the doctor was saying. "It looks like a fine one." His hands were busy.

Jill wanted to look at the colt, but her eyes were too blurred to see. She didn't dare trust her voice to speak. Instead, she turned and walked to the end of the barn. She needed a minute alone. Looking up through the high window, she saw the last star glimmer faintly in the light of dawn. "It's a new day," she said to herself. "A wonderful day."

Back at Dolly's stall, Jill bent with the others to look at the little mare who lay resting with her baby beside her. The colt was a little chestnut, with a white blaze on his nose.

Dr. Young turned to Jill with a smile. "Have you got a name ready for him?"

Jill took a long breath. "Yes," she said. She looked back toward the window where the sky was growing lighter. "His name is Dawn's Wonder."

They came back to the kitchen for hot coffee. Before Dr. Young left, Jill tried to thank him for all he had done.

"No thanks to me," Dr. Young said with a broad smile. "You and Dolly get the credit, Jill. If you hadn't brought the mare through these last weeks—and if she hadn't been a plucky gal herself—we'd never have made it."

When Jill said good-by to Alex she tried to thank him too, but Alex had pulled on his jacket and was out of the door before she could speak. "I'll be back later today to see how things are going," he called gruffly. "Don't worry, Dolly's going to be O.K."

Jill watched him go, still wishing she could have found the right words to say. She saw him walk across the yard in the early morning light, his head down, his hands thrust in his pockets, his shoulders hunched. She thought how lonely he looked. For a moment Jill wondered whether seeing the new colt had made Alex think of Charger. Maybe he was there when Charger was born, she thought.

How would I feel if I were like Alex? Jill wondered. Suppose I didn't have home and Mommy and Daddy? Or Chuck or Jo-Jo or Dolly—and Dawn? Alex's family must seem terribly far away in Alaska. He hadn't any real home.

And whatever had happened to Charger, Alex must certainly have felt terrible about it.

Another thought struck Jill. Maybe Alex is like the little old lady Carol and I saw in the hospital. Maybe he doesn't mean to be difficult; maybe he's just lonely.

Jill turned away slowly and started upstairs. There were too many questions, and she was much too tired to try to answer them. Someday she might know, if Alex would trust her with the answers.

Jerry Patterson wrote a special news item for the next issue of the *Hoofprint:*

JILL'S NEW . RESPONSIBILITY

A few months ago Jill Miller took on the responsibility of Dolly, a quarter-horse mare in foal. We all knew it was a difficult case, because Dolly had a bad case of the heaves. Last Monday night, however, there was a happy ending to the story, when Dolly gave birth to a strong and sassy young colt named Dawn's Wonder. Jill picked this name seeing as how the young fellow put in his appearance just when dawn was breaking.

With a new baby to take care of, this means, of course NO LOAFING, Jill.

Carol announced at the next Merrymakers' meeting that Kenny Graham's visit had been arranged. There was great excitement planning to entertain the lad from Michigan. Kenny was to stay with the Millers. Chuck's room would be empty and, being on the first floor, it would mean no stairs to climb for the sick boy.

"Kenny really isn't sick any more," Carol explained. "But he still has to be careful. His mother says Kenny has been so excited ever since he's known about the visit that he makes plans and asks questions morning, noon, and night. She says he's even started to pack his suitcase three times and she's had to unpack it again."

First of all Kenny was interested in plant culture, so Tim Stanford and Gig Williamson would take him in special charge. Tim and Gig had both had 4-H grain projects, and they promised to have as much information and as many samples ready for Kenny as they could find. Kenny would see how the rye and barley plants from his own seeds were growing.

"Scotty says we can write to the University," Gig said. "If we tell them about Kenny, they'll answer his questions and tell him about other experiments he can make with plants."

The other Merrymakers had a dozen ideas for entertaining their guest. "He can visit all our homes," they said, "and see our projects."

Carol would call a special Merrymakers' meeting in Kenny's honor.

"I wish it were better weather so we could have a cookout," Jill said, "or as least a picnic."

The He-Man Chefs came to the rescue with a better idea. "We'll have a barbecue in our barn," Tim Stanford said. "Steaks and roast potatoes and pizza on the side. And apple pie and chocolate cake."

"If you have another Dagwood sandwich contest, please be careful." Carol laughed. "We don't want to put Kenny back in the hospital when he's just gotten out!"

By the day of Kenny's arrival, everything was ready. Jill and Jo Ann had fixed up Chuck's room, and they waited eagerly for Kenny. Carol was driving him from the airport and when they saw her car turn in the drive, the girls went out to meet their guest.

Kenny was a small boy for his age, and thin. But there was a bright color in his cheeks and a sparkle in his eyes that made him seem as lively as any of them. By dinnertime all the Millers felt that Kenny was a member of the family. The only problem was to keep them all from talking to Kenny at once. They each wanted to tell him everything.

Kenny was amazingly quick at making friends, with animals as well as people. The puppy, Wishbone, had taken just one look at Kenny and claimed the boy for his own. Wherever Kenny went, Wishbone followed, staying as close as possible and wriggling with happiness whenever Kenny patted him. "I've never had a dog," Kenny said. "I wonder how Wishbone knows I've always wanted one."

"Maybe because Wishbone has always wanted a master." Mrs. Miller smiled.

Kenny was taken to see the Millers' barn and the cattle. He paid a special visit to Dolly and Dawn. Dawn was growing into a sturdy little colt. He stood very straight beside his mother and came over to be petted when Jill showed Kenny how to coax him with a carrot to eat. Dawn nuzzled the boy's hand with his velvety nose.

"He tickles." Kenny laughed.

The next day Kenny's tour began, as one Merrymaker after another took him to visit and showed him their livestock. They pointed out their crop projects and explained the soil conservation they had studied in 4-H.

"I just hope they don't wear the boy out," Mrs. Miller said a little anxiously.

But Kenny loved every minute. The first feeling of spring was in the wind, and as they drove beside the miles of wheat fields, just beginning to show pale green, Kenny lifted his head and breathed as though he could never get his fill of the fresh, sunny air.

"Kenny just loves being outdoors," Jill told Sally. "And at home he never can be, Carol says. He's crazy about plants and flowers and animals, and everything that grows."

"I know." Sally nodded. "He's crazy about 4-H, too. He's interested in absolutely everything the club does and Scotty says the work he's done with plants—just in the window boxes he has at home—is remarkable. Scotty said one of the professors at the University read Kenny's letter explaining how he was trying to develop new plants strains. The professor was so interested that he asked Kenny to write to him again. I just wish Kenny could live here and be a Merrymaker!"

There was no hope of Kenny staying in Dale Valley, but the evening before he had to leave for home, the Merrymakers held a special meeting for him. They put on their best demonstrations for Kenny, and sang their favorite 4-H songs.

Then Carol asked Kenny to tell them about his special work with plant culture.

Kenny stood up and faced the audience as calmly as though he had been making speeches all his life. He explained how better plants and bigger grain or vegetables or flowers could come from putting different plant varieties together, and trying to develop the best qualities of each strain. He told how the great naturalist, Luther Burbank, had begun the work, and how it had become a science.

"The work is never finished," Kenny said. "There are

always ways to keep improving plants and seeds—and that's the kind of work I'd like best of anything to do someday, if I can learn enough about it to get a job."

Kenny ended his speech with his thanks to the Merrymakers. "I guess there isn't any way to really thank you, but I'll just say I never, never knew there was as much fun in the whole world as I've had here."

As Kenny sat down, Gig Williamson's long arm shot up.

"Madam Carol, I mean, Madam President," Gig began, trying to speak loudly enough to be heard above the applause that followed Kenny's speech, "I want to say something. I guess I mean I want to make a motion. I move that Kenny be made a member of the Merrymakers even if he doesn't live here. I move we make him an honorary member."

At least a dozen voices seconded the motion. It was unanimously carried. When Kenny stood up, looking surprised and pleased, everyone clapped again.

The He-Man barbecue that followed the meeting finished off Kenny's visit with a crashing success. When it came to the Dagwood sandwiches, Kenny astonished everyone by building the most magnificent one of all. Hamburger, peanut butter, chili sauce, and lettuce were topped off by sardines, bacon, and cheese. While the Merrymakers stared, wide-eyed, Kenny reached over, calmly added a sprinkling of nuts, and topped it with a maraschino cherry.

The whole group broke into cheers as Kenny took a He-Man-size bite, swallowed it, and grinned.

Saying good-night later, they called last messages to Kenny.

"We'll write you, and you write us—"

"Come back soon—"

"And remember, you're a Merrymaker now—"

"It's been wonderful having Kenny here, and I'll miss him," Mrs. Miller said, when they were at home again. Kenny was asleep, with Wishbone curled on the foot of his bed as he had been every night of Kenny's visit. "The only thing that worries me is that poor puppy. Wishbone hasn't let Kenny out of his sight since the boy got here. I'm afraid it will break both their hearts when they have to say good-by tomorrow."

"I have an idea," Jo Ann said suddenly. "Why don't we give Wishbone to Kenny to take home? Wishbone's such a polite dog, I'll bet he wouldn't mind one bit being house-broken to an apartment."

"Especially if he could stay with Kenny," Jill added.

It was decided then and there. When Kenny drove off with Carol the next morning, Wishbone sat beside him on the seat. Cindy's old collar was around the puppy's neck. And Jo Ann had lent Kenny her best red leather belt to use for a leash.

"I thought I'd die if Kenny had to leave all by himself," Jill said, waving one last time, as the car disappeared onto the highway. "But now that he has Wishbone with him, I know they'll both be all right."

CHAPTER 12

Call in the Night

"If I could just decide whether to have a checked dress with plain collar and cuffs, or a plain dress with checked collar and cuffs," Jo Ann sighed one morning at breakfast. "Mrs. Stanford says we have to choose today, and I just can't."

Jo Ann and Dot were choosing materials for their 4-H sewing project. It was the first time either of them had attempted a dress. They planned to have them ready for Easter Sunday, and they had agonized for days over samples and patterns.

"It's just making a wreck of me," Jo Ann said, putting an extra spoonful of brown sugar on her bowl of oatmeal and cream.

"At least it hasn't wrecked your appetite," her father said unsympathetically. "If you can't make up your mind what you want, why not flip a coin?"

Jo Ann made no reply. She tried to look as dignified and wounded as possible, in spite of her mouth being very full.

The great decision was finally made. The materials and patterns were bought, and for the next week the girls worked frantically. Their families grew accustomed to stepping over cloth, pincushions, and scissors on the living-room floor.

"It's a wonder we haven't all got blood poisoning from walking on needles and pins," Jill said.

With last-minute help from Mrs. Stanford at an emergency meeting of the sewing group, the girls managed to finish their dresses in time to wear on Easter Sunday. Jo Ann's navy checked taffeta looked crisp and fresh with a white collar and a red belt to match the red headband on her dark hair. Dot wore her gray jumper with a white blouse, a round white sailor hat with red streamers, and new red flats. Their mothers had given them each new white purses and gloves.

"Jo-Jo and Dot really do look darling," Jill whispered to her mother on the way into church, "but I just hope they won't explode with pride during the service!"

Jill and Sally had saved their money from baby-sitting to buy new clothes for themselves. Sally had a navy blue and white coat and dress, Jill had a blue dress with a deeper blue jacket that matched her eyes.

After church, the Merrymakers gathered at the hospital to bring Easter baskets to the patients. Jill and Carol had a pink hyacinth plant for Mrs. D. The nurse on the corridor gave the girls a welcoming grin. "Every time you two come to see Mrs. D. it puts her in a better mood," the nurse said. "I won't say she's a lamb, but at least she's less ferocious for a day or two."

The Millers had hardly recovered from the flurry of Jo-Jo's sewing before she decided on a new project. She wanted to give a demonstration of making an angel-food cake for 4-H Achievement Day, when members from each club in the county would show their best skills.

With her mother as teacher and audience, Jo-Jo stood

at the kitchen table, mixing bowls, ingredients, and electric beater ready before her. "To make an angel food cake," she started brightly, "we begin by separating ten eggs. . . ."

More than an hour later, when Jill came in from the barn after taking care of Dolly and Dawn, she found her mother still sitting at the table. Jo-Jo was putting aside another demonstration cake. Her cheeks were flushed, there was a streak of flour on her nose. A small mountain of eggshells was piled on the table.

"Try once more," Mrs. Miller was saying patiently. "Remember to whip in the sugar little by little, and remember that to give a good demonstration you must explain each step *as you go along*. Keep talking."

"When I talk I forget to work," Jo Ann wailed, "and when I keep my mind on what I'm doing, I can't remember to talk! But I'll get this right if I have to break every egg in the state of Kansas." She rinsed the bowls, composed her face into a gracious smile, and started again. "To make an angel food cake, we begin by separating ten eggs. . . ."

By Achievement Day Jo Ann was ready to represent the Merrymakers with her demonstration. The Millers' deep freeze was filled with enough practice cakes to last the family for six months. "And my poor chickens have eaten eggshells until they have enough calcium to turn them to stone." Mrs. Miller laughed. "At least," she added, "it isn't as bad as the time Chuck was going to give a demonstration of how to wire a doorbell. He had wires strung all over the house and we didn't dare touch anything for fear of being electrocuted."

The last of Jo Ann's practice cakes was served for dessert that evening. "Light as a feather, Jo-Jo," her father said, swallowing the final bite. "Make one this good in your demonstration tomorrow and the Merrymakers will bring home the angel-food honors."

Jo Ann shook her head wearily. "I don't know why they call it angel food," she said. "If angels have as much trouble baking it as I did, I hope I'm never a cook in heaven!"

Jo-Jo did carry off her demonstration well, and the other Merrymakers represented the club with honors.

Carol was proud of them all. "I just wish Johnny could have seen you," she said.

When the Millers pulled into their driveway, they were startled to hear the telephone ringing in the dark house.

"I wonder who could be calling this late." Mrs. Miller looked anxious.

Jill hopped out of the back seat and ran to answer. A minute later she was back. "Daddy, it's for you." Her voice sounded frightened. "Dr. Bartlett is calling from the Lanes' house. He wants you right away."

When Mr. Miller turned back from the telephone his face was grave. "There's bad news," he said. "Bert Lane has had a heart attack and Dr. Bartlett is afraid he may not pull through. I'm going over right away. Johnny's mother and Deedee are there alone. They've telephoned Johnny at the University, but it'll be at least three or four hours before he can get home."

Mrs. Miller and the two girls stood stunned by the news. It seemed impossible to think that Johnny's father, who always seemed so big and healthy, might be dying. "Oh, poor Edith," Mrs. Miller said in distress. "I'll go with you, Tom, and help any way I can. You girls will be all right here." She turned to give Jill and Jo Ann a quick kiss. "Take care of things. I'll call you as soon as there's any news."

When the car had gone, Jill looked at her sister. She saw that there were tears on Jo-Jo's cheeks and that she was trembling. Suddenly Jill felt very grown up and responsible. "Come out to the kitchen, Jo-Jo," she said, trying to sound just like her mother. She put her arm around Jo Ann and was surprised to find how childish the thin little shoulders felt. In the kitchen she made hot milk and Jo-Jo's favorite cinnamon toast. She was touched by the trusting way Jo Ann's eyes followed her and by the way the younger girl sipped the hot drink and ate her toast obediently. When they had finished and turned out the kitchen light, Jo Ann followed Jill upstairs.

"Jill, would you mind very much if I slept in your room tonight?" Jo-Jo asked. "It's not that I'm scared or anything, it's just that I keep thinking—" The small voice broke and she turned suddenly to put her arms around Jill's neck. "Oh, Jill, suppose something like this happened to Daddy or Mommy. . . ."

The telephone call came just as the girls were getting breakfast the next morning. Mr. Lane had died. Johnny had managed to get there just in time to see his father before it was too late. "I don't know when we can get home, honey," Mrs. Miller told Jill. "We'll stay here and help as long as we're needed."

"Don't worry, we're all right," Jill answered. She looked at her sister over the telephone. "Jo-Jo's just fine. She and I can do everything here. Tell Daddy I got out to the barn early and did most of the chores. I can finish before time for the school bus."

86

As Jill filled the thermos bottles and packed their lunches for school, she tried to keep up cheerful conversation for Jo Ann. But one thought kept going round and round in her mind.

"What will this mean to Johnny and Carol, and all the plans they've made together?"

Johnny's brother Bill was still in the Army, stationed somewhere in Japan. Until Bill got home, there was only Johnny's mother, and fourteen-year-old Deedee, to run the ranch. Would it mean that Johnny would have to leave college and give up his plans for medical school? Slapping together a peanut-butter sandwich, Jill sent up a silent, desperate prayer. "*Please make it all right for Carol and Johnny. Please, please, make it all right.*"

On the school bus Jill and Sally talked about the news in hushed, shocked voices. "It'll just kill Carol and Johnny if Johnny has to give up being a doctor," Sally whispered. "But I heard Dad say this morning he was afraid Johnny wouldn't even be able to stay at college to graduate."

"I'd give anything in the world if there were something we could do to help." Jill nodded. "But I can't imagine what it would be."

By that evening there was a telegram that Johnny's brother Bill had emergency leave and was flying home. When he came, there was a council at the Lane House.

When Mr. Miller came home he went straight to the telephone to call Scotty and explain what had happened. The situation looked just about hopeless for Johnny, Mr. Miller said, unless something could be done quickly. Johnny's brother Bill had only a few days' leave from the Army. It would be another two years before Bill's Army service was finished. That meant Johnny would have to stay home and take care of the ranch until Bill could return.

"There's no way around that fact that we can see," Mr. Miller told Scotty on the telephone. "It means Johnny can't go on to medical school in the fall. But there may be a way that Johnny can stay and graduate from college in June. That is, if you think we can swing it."

The plan, Mr. Miller explained to Scotty, was to get the Merrymakers together, with any parents who could help, and keep the ranch going for Mrs. Lane these next two months until Johnny graduated.

"It will be a big responsibility," Mr. Miller told Scotty. "There are the barns and forty head of cattle to take care of, and the sheep, and there'll be hay to cut before the middle of June. But if the Merrymakers are willing to pitch in—and if you'll back us—I believe we can do it."

Jill overheard the conversation and her heart pounded with excitement. The moment her father left the telephone she ran to throw her arms around him. "Daddy, what a perfectly wonderful plan! With all of us working, we'll take care of the ranch until Johnny graduates. What did Scotty say? Can we do it?"

"Scotty's coming down to talk it over," Mr. Miller said. "We'll call a special meeting of the Merrymakers to decide."

Before Bill Lane flew back to Japan, the plans were made. The Merrymakers had voted to take over the job of running the Lane ranch. Scotty worked out a schedule with them, giving each member a share of the work, and a definite time to do it.

"This is a big job, even for 4-H'ers," Mr. Miller reminded

them soberly. "Scotty and your leaders will help as much as they can, but most of the work will be up to you youngsters."

When Johnny heard the news that he would be able to stay at college until graduation, he said slowly, "I've heard of a friend in need, but I never heard of so many friends in need." He looked around at the Merrymakers. "I'll never forget what you're doing," he said.

"I was so afraid Johnny might give up his dream of going to medical school when this happened," Sally told Jill. "But Carol wouldn't let him."

"The only difference in our plans is time," Carol had told Johnny. Her eyes were as steady and sure as ever. "It will take longer than we thought, but I'm going to be a nurse and you're going to be a doctor—and I'll wait for you. You and I are doing this together, Johnny."

"Carol was wonderful," Jill said. "So was Johnny. All I hope in my whole life is that someday I'll feel about somebody the way Johnny and Carol do about each other."

The next weeks were busy ones for the Merrymakers. They all had chores of their own to do, and their school-

work. Helping at the Lane ranch meant getting up extra early in the morning, or giving up free time in the afternoons and evenings. But they kept their schedule somehow.

"I just hope the Lord isn't keeping a record of the Merrymakers' complaints this month," Jill said on a particularly rainy and discouraging Saturday morning. She was due at the Lane ranch by seven o'clock—it was the day when the sheep were to be dipped, and she could imagine herself pushing one fat, furry rump after another down the chute.

The Merrymakers kept their promise. The Lane cattle were fed, the cows milked, and the fields in order. They planted the vegetable garden and even found time to make a flower bed for Mrs. Lane. Scotty helped as much as he could. Mr. Miller and the other 4-H leaders worked with them. And Deedee, Johnny's younger sister, worked as hard as anyone.

"Deedee's a born farmer," Jill heard her father say.

The week Johnny was taking final examinations, the Merrymakers brought in the first crop of hay at the Lane ranch. They were all there to help. Deedee drove the tractor, with the hay baler attached. She sat perched on the high seat, wearing blue jeans and a wide hat, and drove across the fields under the clear blue sky of early June.

The next week Johnny graduated from college.

Jill and her family, with most of the other Merrymakers, had driven over for commencement. When Johnny stepped up to take his diploma, they all clapped. Later he kissed his mother and Deedee, and then Carol, and he was smiling as he shook hands with them all. But Jill saw how serious Johnny's eyes were, in spite of his smile. He seemed to have grown older in the weeks since his father had died. He must be thinking of his father today, Jill realized, and he must be wondering what the future held for Carol and him.

On the trip home, as they drove past mile after mile of ripening wheat fields that rippled gently in the soft evening air, Jill was quiet herself. The older I get, the more happy things seem to get mixed up with sad ones, she thought. I just wish life would stay more simple!

CHAPTER 13

Golden Harvest

By the last week in June the wheat was ripe. The tall stalks were heavy with grain, and the fields glowed like melted gold under the blazing sun.

Harvest days were the most important ones of the whole year on the wheat ranches. Everyone watched the weather. Everyone was a little nervous. They knew they were working against time. One bad storm or a soaking rain, before the grain was in, could ruin a year's crop.

The Miller family all worked together.

Mr. Miller and Chuck were up at daylight and in the fields. "I wanted to hire Alex to help," Mr. Miller said, "but he's taken a job at the feed store in Dale Valley for the summer. Ed Marshall says the boy even works overtime to earn as much money as he can."

Jill and Jo Ann and Mrs. Miller followed the men into the fields as soon as they had cleared the table after the hearty breakfast. Sally and Jerry came over to work for the week—they were free to help since the Pattersons raised mainly cattle and had no big wheat harvest to bring in.

The last helper on the Miller ranch was Larry Stevens, who had been Chuck's roommate at the University. Larry surprised them by driving in unexpectedly from Wichita.

"If you want a city slicker to get in your way, here I am," Larry announced cheerfully, heaving his suitcase out of the car. "Chuck kept telling me all year that anybody with two arms and legs and no more than two heads was welcome as extra help on harvest days. So I thought I'd come over and find out whether he meant it. Just tell me what mistakes to make, and I promise to make 'em."

Larry's welcome from the Millers was as cordial as Chuck had promised. After the first half-hour, Larry caught on surprisingly well. He worked steadily, never complaining, even though his face and shoulders burned lobster red under the broiling sun. Mr. Miller found an old, wide-brimmed straw hat for Larry to wear.

"Now you look more like a farmer than any of us," Mr. Miller said, as Larry slapped the hat on the back of his head and mopped his fiery face.

Before the week was over, Larry was completely at home.

One night when Sally was staying at the Millers', she and Jill had a confidential talk about Larry.

"He's different from any boy I've ever known," Sally said. "Only not different the way Alex is—"

"Oh, not a bit," Jill agreed. "Of course, I know Larry is miles too old for me. But sometimes he smiles at me and talks to me as though he were really noticing me."

"He does at me, too," Sally said.

They both sighed.

On the last day of the harvest the morning dawned with a bright, hot sun. By noon, however, a dark bank of clouds hung over the horizon.

As they hurried through dinner at noon, forks of lightning

streaked through the sky. Mr. Miller looked worried. "I'm afraid that storm is going to get ahead of us," he said. "We'll have to work as fast as we can if we hope to finish in time."

They were hardly back in the fields before a car came zooming up the drive. Johnny Lane jumped out. "I don't know whether you need an extra hand or not," he said, "but if you do, here I am." His own wheat was already in, Johnny said. "Carol told me you were still working. When I saw the storm coming up, I knew you'd be racing to finish before it struck."

With Johnny's skillful help they could work faster.

In the last hour, with the sky growing still blacker, another car skidded up to the house, and Alex hurried toward them. Alex had seen the storm, too. He had taken time from his job in Dale Valley and come to help in the last frantic race.

No one paused for greetings. Before Alex could speak, Mr. Miller had shouted an order to him. Every second was precious now. They worked together, no one speaking, each face grimly determined, until the last grain was stored. Chuck drove the tractor into the barn just as a crash of thunder seemed to explode above their heads. The next moment the rain poured down.

"We've made it!" Mr. Miller called. "Run for the house, everyone!"

They raced across the yard and crowded into the kitchen, drenched and breathless. Jill was the last one in. She slammed the door against a furious gust of rain. "Go ahead and howl," she said to the storm outside. "We don't care now. We're safe!"

"Whew! That was a photo finish." Larry grinned as Mrs. Miller handed him a cup of hot coffee. "Chuck didn't tell me that harvesting a wheat crop is more exciting than a western movie. I'll never look at another slice of bread without thinking how somebody must have raced to bring in the wheat to make the flour to bake the bread!"

Mr. Miller laughed. "We don't guarantee chills and thrills with every harvest," he said. "Most years it's just plain hard work, and no excitement." He paused and looked toward the window. Beyond the streaming pane, the fields lay bare under the crashing storm. Where the wheat had stood tall and golden a week before, there were only rows of stubble. "Just the same," he finished, "a farmer has one satisfaction. He can *see* a year's work done."

The Millers coaxed Larry to stay on a few days longer. "You've worked so hard with us," they said. "At least stay and let us show you a little fun."

There was a picnic on the Fourth of July.

"We set off half the fireworks to celebrate Independence Day, and the other half to celebrate getting in the harvest," Jill explained to Larry.

The next day they took Larry for a swim at the Dale Valley pool, then around to visit the other farms and ranches.

The Merrymakers were already beginning to get their projects ready to show at the Dale County Fair, which would be held in August.

"They don't have 4-H where I live," Larry said. "But just watching you, I'm beginning to feel that old 4-H spirit myself."

Another big event was to come before the fair. The summer 4-H camp was at Rock Springs. Going to camp was the high spot of the year for every 4-H member. Each county was given certain dates to send campers. But when Scotty

announced that the Merrymakers' dates were in mid-July,
Jill collapsed with a groan.

"I can't go then because the Gibsons are going away that
week," she wailed, "and I've promised to stay and help the
grandmother take care of the children!" The Gibsons were
Jill's best baby-sitting customers. "I can't disappoint them,"
she said. "But I've missed Rock Springs so often it just isn't
fair. Once it was because I had the mumps, and once because of my cousin's wedding; and last year we were away
visiting relatives. Oh, *darn*," she finished disgustedly.

The next morning Jill was putting Dawn through his
paces, practicing for the fair, when she looked up to see
Larry watching.

Alex had marked out a ring. He had taught Jill just how
to lead Dawn at a walk and trot, to show his gaits, then
to make him "park" or "stretch" and stand quietly. "That's
so the judge can see the colt's conformation," Jill explained
to Larry. "It's the hardest part for Dawn to learn. If only

he would behave as well as Dolly! But he just hates to stand still."

The colt had grown and developed beautifully. He stood on straight, slender legs; his chestnut coat gleamed like dark satin; and the white blaze was a snowy streak down his nose. He had his mother's quick, graceful ways, but not her shy gentleness. He was as curious as a monkey. His sharp ears were always pricked up for a new sound. There was an imp of mischief in his bright eyes.

After an hour of working with the colt, Jill was tired out. Dearly as she loved Dawn, she was ready to spank his little rump for not behaving better. When she walked over to Larry, he was smiling.

"Alex says he expects that little horse of yours to win something at the fair," Larry said. "I'll bet he's right. Anyway, I'll be cheering for you, gal."

Jill stopped short in amazement at Larry's words. In all the months she had worked over Dolly and Dawn, Alex had never told her she was doing well. With all the patient hours of help Alex had given her, he hadn't spoken a single word of praise.

Yet Larry, in one casual remark, had given her just the encouragement she needed. Jill lifted her shoulders. All her tiredness was gone. Larry's words made her want to work harder than ever.

Leading Dawn back to the barn, Jill was still puzzled. All Alex's work couldn't have helped her more than what Larry had said in one minute. But Larry's words couldn't have helped her without all that Alex had done.

If I live to be a hundred, Jill thought, I'll never understand how people can be so different.

CHAPTER 14

Campfire

While Sally and the other Merrymakers made their plans for going to camp, Jill sat by, morosely listening. She sighed long sighs and felt extremely sorry for herself. It wasn't fair that she had worked harder for 4-H this year than she ever had in her life, and still she had to miss the fun of Rock Springs, she told herself resentfully.

Just four days before the Rock Springs trip, the Millers were at the dinner table when the telephone rang. Jill went to answer.

It was Mrs. Gibson calling. The two babies were sick with mumps, she told Jill. Their trip was postponed, and they wouldn't need Jill to stay at the house until later in the month.

Jill came back to the table dancing a wild Highland fling. *"Hurray, hurray, hurray,* HURRAY! The Gibsons have the mumps TODAY," she chanted. *"And I don't have to go and* STAY!"

"You shouldn't feel glad when someone else has bad luck," Jo Ann said primly, "or at least you shouldn't say it out loud."

"I don't see why," Jill answered. "I had the mumps myself and they weren't so very awful. And if I don't have to go to the Gibsons, it means I *can* go to camp with Sally and you and the others."

"Now, wait a minute, Jilly. Wait a minute." Mr. Miller put up his hand. "This is a pretty late date to try to get a place for you at Rock Springs. The camp reservations have been in long ahead of time."

"Oh, Daddy—" Jill's face went from smiles to tragedy. "You don't mean that there wouldn't be room for me! You don't mean now that I *can* go to camp, maybe I can't!"

She clasped her hands and her voice rose in a wail.

"For heaven's sake, Jill, stop acting like the dying swan," her father said. "Nobody's saying you can't go, but I'll have to call Scotty right away and find out whether they'll have room to take you."

Jill paced the floor while her father made the call. When he came back into the room he was laughing. "It's all right, Jill. Scotty says there'll be a place for you at Rock Springs. And wait until you hear the reason." He stopped Jill as she rushed to give him a hug. "There's a vacancy at camp because Scotty just got a telephone call canceling a reservation. Someone just came down with mumps!"

Nearly all the Merrymakers were going to Rock Springs except Alex. "Scotty offered Alex a chance to go," Jill told Sally, "but he said he couldn't afford to take time away from his job in Dale Valley."

"Sometimes I think Alex just doesn't like to have fun," Sally said.

Jill nodded doubtfully. "Or maybe he needs the money for something we don't know about."

The first sight Jill and Sally had of Rock Springs was when Scotty's station wagon swung off the highway onto a private road. They saw the camp gates and, just inside, the original house where the family that first owned Rock Springs had lived. Beside the white house the spring gushed past—a rush of clear, sparkling water that turned a huge, wooden mill wheel round and round.

The girls, with their duffels and bedrolls slung over their shoulders, stopped to listen to the splashing water and the soft creak of the old wheel.

"It must be the coolest sound in the world," Jill said. She drew a deep breath. "And to think how long the spring has been turning that wheel." She looked up at the side of the hill behind the house, where the water poured from a dark opening in the side of the hill.

"Scotty says the spring must have been there thousands of years," Sally said. "He says the water never stops coming, no matter how dry a summer is. Nobody knows where it starts from, maybe from some underground lake that's hundreds of feet deep, he said. That's what the Indians who used to live here believed. They even made up legends about the buried lake and the spirits that were in it. Anyway, the water just pours and pours out of the side of the hill."

"Hey, what gives? Are you two turning into water nymphs or something?" A voice just behind them made the girls jump. They turned to see Jerry and Tim, who had driven over with Mr. Patterson.

"We were just watching the spring, wondering where it comes from," Jill said. "The Indians thought there was an underground lake haunted with spirits, or something."

Jerry shook his head. "If the mystery goes back that far, you might as well stop trying to solve it now. Scotty says to find your tents and get unpacked as fast as you can. There'll be a free swim for everybody before lunch."

The girls wasted no time. They raced down the line of tents in the girls' camping area, found Number 15, and put their duffels on the last two vacant bunks. The other girls had already arrived, and there was a flurry of introductions.

"I'm Ellie Mae Lamb from Marsh County," a girl with bright red curls and a turned-up nose said. "Sally and Jill, this is Fran and Mary and Bonnie. I know we're going to be the best friends in the whole world," she went on, pulling up the straps of her bathing suit, "but I just heard someone say there's a swim before lunch and right now let's head for that great big pool and get coo-ool! Bye, Jill! Bye, Sally! Bye, everybody! I'll see you on the diving board." Ellie Mae snatched up her bathing cap and towel and disappeared. The other girls hurried to follow.

The pool was the biggest Jill had ever seen. They raced each other to splash into the clear, blue water and came up spluttering.

"The water's icy, but it feels wonderful." Jill shivered deliciously. She and Sally saw Jerry and Tim dive from the far end of the pool and swam out to meet them. "We'll race you three times the length," Jill called, "and whoever comes in last is a three-toed, yellow-bellied platypus."

After lunch in the dining-hall building, Jill went on a tour of the camp. She saw the athletic fields and the council circle, the chapel and the Health Center and the auditorium. She heard how, years ago, the very first money to buy the property for a camp had been money 4-H members raised themselves, bit by bit, by doing odd jobs and holding cake sales. Gradually the funds had grown, and with the help of generous gifts, the project had grown to the beautiful camp she saw now.

Everywhere Jill went she met campers from other parts of the state. Two girls in Indian saris passed her in the auditorium, and Jill knew these were among the visitors from other countries of the world who exchanged places with American 4-H'ers. Each camper she passed had a friendly smile or greeting that made Jill feel at home.

Every moment of the days at Rock Springs was full of excitement.

A high spot of the camping days was riding the beautiful palomino horses over the trails. Jill and Jerry had visited the big stables the first thing. They went up and down the long rows of stalls, stopping to make friends with each horse, coaxing them over to pat soft noses.

"These horses really live it up," Jerry said. He looked at the big, light barn, the comfortable box stalls, the high lofts filled with hay bales. "I just wish Blackjack had half as nice a place."

"I wish Dolly and Dawn had, too." Jill nodded. "Our barn at home is pretty nice, but this is really super horse luxury." She stroked a horse's cheek and the familiar feel made her suddenly homesick for Dawn and Dolly. "I hope Daddy remembers to keep Dolly's hay damp and fix her mash just the way I showed him," she said.

Riding over the trails, coming back when the late-afternoon shadows were falling across the hills, Jill forgot everything except the wide, beautiful country. Ellie Mae rode close beside her. "I've never been on a horse before," Ellie Mae had said before they started. "I'm just scared to death one will start to rear up the way Silver does with the Lone Ranger on TV." For the first half of the ride Ellie Mae clung to the pommel of the saddle for dear life and squealed every time her horse moved faster than a slow walk. Now, on the way home, she sat easily and handled her reins like a veteran rider.

"I don't know why I ever was afraid of this little old horse." Ellie Mae patted her palomino's mane. "He's just an apple dumpling, that's what he is. I can't wait to tell Daddy I've learned how to ride."

Jill lifted her face to the golden sky. "It's funny—we've only been here a few days," she said dreamily, "but it's been so wonderful, I feel as though I'd lived a whole life at Rock Springs."

There was a barbecue picnic and an amateur show that night. Long tables, set out under the early-evening sky, were loaded with food. Jill, standing in line with Sally and Ellie Mae and Jerry and Tim, sniffed the delicious smell of roast meat.

The talent contest came after supper. Some of the campers, who had studied music, sang or played a solo instrument. Others had gotten up comedy skits or sketches to act out. There were several quartets—Jill and Ellie Mae sang in one, accompanied by a boy with a guitar.

"You were even on the air," Sally told Jill after the performance. The local broadcasting station had sent a sound truck to pick up parts of the program. "I saw them recording while your quartet was singing," Sally said. "Scotty says the program will be on the air tomorrow. I heard him give the radio man your names, and when he came to Jill Miller, the man said, 'That's the cute gal with the pony tail. She's got a nice voice, too.' Maybe somebody will discover you're a great singer and you'll be another Patti Page."

"Or Rosemary Clooney," Jill said.

They were both laughing. But a sudden thought struck Jill. If she had heard someone say that a year ago, she would have immediately imagined herself as a star. She would have raced off on a new ambition of being a radio singer. Now she went more slowly. She knew dreams were wonderful. But she had begun to realize how much work went into a dream before it could come true.

Candlelight vesper service, on the last evening, was held around the council fire. Sitting in the circle of stone seats where so many 4-H campers had sat before them, each with a lighted candle, they watched the flames leap from the fire in the center.

Closing the service, they all stood up together to sing the 4-H hymn. Then a tall girl with a clear, sweet voice sang "Taps."

"Day is done,
"Gone the sun,
"From the lake, from the hills, from the sky.
"All is well;
"Safely rest,
"God is nigh."

The last note faded into silence. For a minute there was only the faint crackle of the dying fire and the flickering candle flames.

Then one by one the candles went out, and the campers moved away in groups of twos and threes. As they walked back to their tents for the last time, their voices were quiet, hushed by the spell of the stars and the soft summer night.

Ellie Mae linked arms with Jill and Sally. "You're the two best friends I've ever had," she said. "I'm so glad you've invited me to come and spend Thanksgiving vacation at Dale Valley. If I thought we'd never see each other after tomorrow, I'd plain die. Anyway, I'll never forget our being here at Rock Springs together."

"Neither will I," Jill echoed. She took a long breath. "I'll never forget one single minute of being here—not as long as I live."

CHAPTER **15**

"Tears into Smiles"

The last two weeks before the Dale County Fair were tense ones for the Merrymakers. They spent every minute getting their exhibits ready.

One evening Mr. Miller came home with the news that Alex had entered a class in horsemanship. "Alex hadn't been sure that Laddie's lame leg would be well enough. But now he's decided to ride."

"I just hope he gets a ribbon," Jill said. "He certainly deserves to, after the way he's worked. If the judges could only see a 'before and after' picture of Laddie, they'd realize what a wonderful job Alex has done."

Alex said nothing. But he worked over Laddie for hours at a time, grooming the palomino to perfection, and schooling him to perfect riding manners.

Other Merrymakers were busy watering vegetables, putting up jams and preserves, fattening hogs and calves and sheep, and sewing. Lois Barnes was fattening her sheep; her brother George was building a pen for his pheasants. "Tim Stanford is going to show a pair of his badgers," Mr. Miller said. "He's one Merrymaker who's sure to bring home a blue ribbon. I doubt if there'll be another badger entered at the fair!"

The next morning Jill and Sally were in the barn early. Sally had spent the night at the Millers'. Now she was helping Jill by brushing and currying Dolly, while Jill trimmed the colt's hoofs the way Alex had taught her.

"You're going to have to come over and help me with my chores later," Sally said. "I promised Daddy I'd be home in time to take care of Cuddles and Pete." She shook her head. "That Pete is a problem child if there ever was one! I've been training and training him to walk with a show halter, and he won't learn. Cuddles follows me like a lamb, but Pete braces his four feet and won't do one single thing I want him to. I'll just die if Pete disgraces me at the fair."

Jill laughed. "Oh, stop sounding like such a worried mother," she said. "You're always fretting about Pete's manners."

"Me a worried mother?" Sally stopped currying and looked up indignantly. "Just listen to who's talking! After the way you've bottle-fed that colt since the minute he was born—" Sally pointed an accusing finger at Dawn's Wonder, who gazed innocently back at her. "You've practically burped him over your shoulder every time he so much as hiccuped! Don't you dare call *me* a nervous mother! That horse baby of yours gets more attention than—than a whole set of quintuplets ever got!"

"Well, of course he does," Jill agreed sweetly. "And he's worth every single minute of it. He's just the most precious, darling, adorable, intelligent, beautiful baby in the whole wide world." Jill leaned over to put her cheek against the colt's neck and let him nuzzle her pony tail. "Now, isn't he?"

"Oh, good grief, you're hopeless." Sally threw down the currycomb and rolled her eyes to heaven. "You sound worse than Jo-Jo talking about Pat Boone."

Scotty warned them all how important it was to show their animals well. "I've seen judges pick a calf or a sheep or a hog for first place," he said, "just because it was shown better than another animal that might be just as good."

"But don't worry too much." Mr. Miller laughed. "Remember the time Gig Williamson's Poland China pig got away and started to eat the judge's hat. He got a blue ribbon anyway. The judge said the pig showed good taste!"

Sally had fattened Cuddles and Pete until they were huge. "Who would ever think they were once the little calves we thought were so cute?" Jill said.

"Daddy says Cuddles and Pete each weigh over one thousand pounds." Sally nodded proudly. "They're even heavier than Hotty and Fatty were."

Just before the fair, the county 4-H clubs had clean-up day, when the fairgrounds, the grandstands, the buildings, and the show ring were put in order, ready for the exhibits. Fathers helped, bringing pick-up trucks, mowers, and rollers for the heavy work. The washing racks were set up, where calves and pigs could be given their last-minute grooming and scrubbing.

After two days' work the grounds were ready. The 4-H'ers celebrated with a picnic and a swim in the park pool. "Oh, but it feels wonderful to be cool again!" Jo Ann splashed into the water and rolled over to float on her back, looking up at the August sky above. "I just hope we all win everything at the fair, especially Jill and Sally and Jerry and Alex and me."

All exhibits for the fair had to be in place by noon the next day.

Starting at dawn, when the air was soft and cool with early-morning shadows, the trucks and cars began to arrive. Displays of canned goods, preserves, vegetables, and quilts were put out. Animals of every description were unloaded and led into pens or stalls. Crates of squawking chickens were set up in the poultry barn. Rabbits, guinea pigs, pheasants, and chinchillas were ready to show. One girl from the Sunflower Club brought a pair of shaggy little Shetland ponies, and Tim's badgers were given a place of honor. Exhibitors roamed about, looking at each other's entries and calculating their chances for a prize from the judges.

Groups of younger 4-H'ers were busy setting up their special booth exhibits in the 4-H building. The Merrymakers had chosen to make an exhibit on soil conservation. Jill and Sally stopped to help the younger ones put the last touches on the booth. Then they took time to cool off with bottles of iced pop. Wandering along, drinks in hand, they stopped to talk with old friends from other 4-H clubs.

With people and cars moving in, the fair grounds were a bustle of activity. Everybody was hurrrying—shouting directions, helping each other lead animals or carry heavy exhibits. Music from the merry-go-round mingled with the voices. A Ferris wheel turned round and round. There was sawdust on the ground and the smell of popcorn was in the air.

Sally and Jill stopped to buy hot dogs and sticks of cotton candy and roamed on, taking bites first from one and then the other.

"Aren't fairs wonderful?" they sighed happily.

A line of 4-H boys and girls waited by the washing racks to groom their calves and hogs and dairy cows. Pigs grunted and calves moo-ed plaintively as they had their feet dunked into soapy pails, and each hoof was carefully polished.

The girls stopped to see Dawn, already in his stall. "I thought Dawn might be nervous, being in a strange place," Jill said. "But he isn't a bit."

The colt didn't look the least bit anxious. He stood with his pert nose over the rail, full of eager curiosity, ready to make friends with every stranger who stopped to pat him.

Pete and Cuddles hadn't arrived yet. Because the midday sun was so hot, a special rule allowed the fat beef calves to be brought in the cooler evening.

Sally had the stall ready for her calves. Jerry had helped her set up a pair of electric fans to keep Pete and Cuddles comfortable. The other 4-H'ers, waiting for their calves to arrive, watched enviously as Jerry demonstrated the home-made cooling system.

"At least Pete and Cuddles won't suffer from the heat the way poor Fat Stuff and Hot Stuff did last year," Sally said. "I'll never forget when Fatty almost fainted while he was being judged. He went down on his knees and I thought I'd never get him up."

As the afternoon wore on, Sally began to watch anxiously for the truck to arrive. "I'll feel better when Pete and Cuddles are actually here," she said. "I'll feel even better tomorrow, when the beef judging is over. No matter how much I look forward to a fair, I always have butterflies in the tummy at the last minute. You're lucky anyway," she told Jill. "You don't have to start worrying about Dawn yet."

Jill shook her head uncertainly. Horse and pony classes were not to be judged until the last day of the fair. "But I can feel the beginning of some tummy butterflies right now," Jill said.

The Merrymakers had done well so far. Their booth exhibit had a third prize, and one of the older girls in Mrs. Stanford's sewing class had won a trophy for her tailored suit in the style show. Jill and Sally were thrilled when they found that the judges had given Jo Ann's angel-food cake a prize, although Jill couldn't hold back a sigh of dismay. "This means Jo-Jo can enter a cake at the State Fair," she groaned. "If she practices baking until then—and feeds us all the cakes—we'll be as fat as pigs!"

The girls had just come out of the 4-H building when Jill suddenly pointed toward the road that led from the fairgrounds' entrance. "There's the truck," she said, through a mouthful of hamburger.

Sally gave a shriek. "Cuddles and Pete are here! I can't wait to see them unloaded."

The girls had started to run when they saw Mr. Patterson coming toward them through the crowd.

"Hi, Dad!" Sally called eagerly. Then something queer in her father's expression made her stop uncertainly.

"Sally," Mr. Patterson began, and his voice sounded queer, too, "I have something to tell you." There was a pause. Mr. Patterson frowned and cleared his throat. "Sally, you've had bad luck. There was an accident in the truck. One of your calves slipped out of his halter and fell. They found him when they started to unload. He's dead, Sally. Cuddles is dead."

For a long moment Sally stared back as if she simply hadn't understood. Then she said quietly, "Oh, no, he isn't, Daddy. Cuddles couldn't possibly be dead."

"Sally, listen to me," her father said again, "I'm terribly sorry, but—" He didn't finish. Sally had walked on past him, toward the place where the truck was unloading.

Jill turned to follow. Like Sally, she couldn't believe what Mr. Patterson had said. But when she saw Sally break into a run, she hurried to keep up.

By the time they reached the truck, neither of the girls had any doubt of what had happened. Big, heavy, beautiful Cuddles was lying limply on the ground. A ring of people stood looking down. They moved aside to let Sally through, and Jill stood beside Sally, wracked with sympathy. Sally bent down, twisting her hands and moaning over and over, "It just can't be my Cuddles. It just can't be—"

Jill heard the truck driver explain what had happened. The calves had been tied inside the truck. When Cuddles had somehow slipped off his halter, the jostling of the truck must have made him lose his footing. He had fallen and the other calves had trampled on him.

"I'm mighty sorry, Miss," the driver said to Sally. "I'd have done anything I could to keep you from losing a fine calf like that. I just hope you don't blame me."

Sally was still crying too hard to answer. She only shook her head.

The circle of people moved aside again to let Mr. Patterson through. There was a familiar figure with him. It was Scotty.

Scotty looked quickly down at Cuddles, then he put his hand on Sally's shoulder. "Sally," he said, "you raised a beautiful calf, and you can be proud of that. It was a bad break to lose him—but it was an accident, and it wasn't anybody's fault."

There was a pause. Sally's sobs quieted under Scotty's hand and the steadiness of his voice.

"Don't forget, though," Scotty went on, "you've got another calf to take care of. Why don't you come along and I'll give you a hand with him?"

Sally nodded, gulping bravely. She followed Scotty, still dabbing at her eyes, to find Pete and put him in his stall. "Of course, I couldn't forget Pete," Sally said. "He's the one I'll have to depend on now."

Before they left the fairgrounds that evening, Jill went to see that Dawn was safely bedded down. She still thought he might be lonesome, his first night away from home, but the little colt refused to feel strange. When he came over to nuzzle Jill's hand, hoping for a carrot, his eyes were bright and his ears were pricked as saucily as ever.

Jill said good-night to Dolly later, in the barn at home. The little mare was restless. "I know, you're missing Dawn," Jill said, as Dolly shook her head and paced the stall uneasily. "You needn't worry about Dawn. *That* young man is just fine!" She reached over to give Dolly's neck a sympathetic pat. "Never worry about men," she told Dolly with a laugh. "It's us women who stay at home and fret!"

It wasn't until the next morning that any of them realized that a newspaper photographer had taken a picture of Sally as she had bent over Cuddles.

There was her picture, right on the front page of the *Dale County Press*, with tears running down her cheeks. The headline underneath said: "HOPES INTO TEARS," and the article began:

4-H'er Sally Patterson of Dale Valley mourned today over the fate of her steer Cuddles, found dead on arrival when the truck was unloaded at the opening of the Dale County Fair. Sally could have been voted "the saddest girl in the world" today after all the work and enthusiasm she had put into raising the fine Hereford for her 4-H project. . . .

"My gosh, you're famous," Sally's brother exclaimed when he read the paper. "I never thought we'd have a cover girl in the family. Can I have your autograph?"

"Oh, stop—" Sally wailed. "First I'm laughing, then I'm crying over poor Cuddles, until I don't know what I'm doing."

That afternoon Sally's other calf, Pete, was judged in the Hereford class. Jill stood, with Jo Ann and her father, in the crowd that gathered to watch the final judging. "Sally's got to win. After what happened to Cuddles, she's just *got* to—" Jill murmured tensely.

"Take it easy, Jilly," her father said. "Remember, this is a beef-cattle county, and the competition is mighty stiff. Look at that Black Angus, for instance"— he nodded toward the calves that were being led into the ring—"and that Shorthorn the red-haired boy has. You won't see better steers anywhere in the state of Kansas."

"Well, *we* know Pete's going to win, don't we, Jill?" Jo-Jo squeezed her sister's hand. Ever since her cake had won a blue ribbon, Jo Ann was determined that every other Merry-maker would have a prize. "Then we can all go to the State Fair together," she said happily.

Mr. Miller was right. The contest for the top-winning steers was a stiff one. Every animal in the ring was an almost perfect specimen of its breed.

It seemed hours to Jill before the judge finally made up his mind, and the field was narrowed down to the Black Angus, the Shorthorn—and Pete.

Now came the final moment. Jill could see Sally's eyes, wide and fixed. She had shown her calf beautifully. Now she stood quietly beside Pete, very self-controlled, but Jill could guess how Sally's heart must be pounding as the judge pinned the Grand Champion rosette on the hefty Black Angus, and Sunflower Club members in the audience broke into wild applause.

The next moment the Merrymakers were clapping as loudly. The judge was putting the second rosette on Pete's halter.

Jill and Jo-Jo hugged each other in excitement.

Sally had won the Reserve Championship.

The next day Sally's picture was on the front page of the *Dale County Press* again, this time standing proudly beside Pete. "TEARS INTO SMILES" the new headline said.

Pretty Sally Patterson, who lost her steer Cuddles in an accident yesterday, is all smiles today as the judge pins the Reserve Champion ribbon on her Hereford, Pete. . . . Interviewed after the judging, Sally wiped away one last tear in memory of Cuddles and then flashed a smile that showed two pretty dimples. "You can say this fair had just about everything in it for me," she said. "I've worked hard with both my calves—and then to lose one was almost too much. But after what happened today, how can I be anything but proud and happy?" Asked whether Reserve Champion Pete would go on to the State Fair, Sally gave us another beaming smile. "After what Pete has done," she said, patting the steer's cheek, "I'll get him to Hutchinson if we both have to walk every inch of the way!". . . Good luck, Pete! Good luck, Sally! Our 4-H'ers are a credit to their leaders, their parents, and their community.

CHAPTER **16**

County Fair

"I just don't think I can stand much more excitement," Jill said the next morning. "If I fly all to pieces like this over other people winning or losing, what in the world will I do when I have to walk out in the ring myself?"

When it was Jill's turn to lead Dawn out before the judges that afternoon, however, Jill felt strangely calm. The moment she heard her number called, she forgot all the hours and weeks and months of effort that had led up to this moment. She forgot that anyone was watching. She forgot everything except the judge's voice telling her first to walk the colt, then to let him trot, then walk again.

Dawn saw a fly buzzing by, and turned his head. Jill felt a flash of impatience, then she remembered what Alex had said. "Dawn's a weanling colt," Alex had warned her, "and weanling colts aren't really horses yet—they're more like puppies. They'll frisk around and buck, and kick their heels and bite each other—they'll do anything except what you want them to. But just be patient. Keep coaxing."

Jill pulled Dawn's halter gently, and brought him back in line. He was doing beautifully. He lifted his feet smartly. He never broke his gait. He held his head high, and his ears pricked sharply. When she brought him around the last time, Jill heard a wave of applause from the audience.

Then the judge called for her to stop, and Jill felt a nervous prickle go up her spine. This was the one command Dawn hated. Cautiously she brought the colt to a stop. Gently she coaxed him into the "stretch" position, just as Alex had taught her to do. He stood still, but Jill saw his nostrils flare and the impish look as he rolled his eyes.

"Stand still. Just stand still," Jill whispered desperately between her teeth.

From the corner of her eye, Jill could see the bay saddle-horse filly next to Dawn standing still as a statue, her neck gracefully arched.

Next in the line, a Tennessee walking-horse colt was poised obediently. Then a palomino stood at attention, his coffee-colored ears alert.

"You've got to behave," Jill murmured in Dawn's ear. "You've just got to."

The judge was walking back and forth, looking over the line of colts. He studied their conformation, looked at their hoofs, and ran his hands over their coats.

Jill had heard the applause, she knew that Dawn had done well. She saw the judge coming to look at Dawn and she held his halter firmly.

Just then, without an instant's warning, Jill felt the halter almost jerked out of her hand. Dawn had flung his head in the air. He was backing away from the judge, snorting and pawing, his eyes rolling.

Jill held on. She ordered Dawn furiously to stop. But even as she struggled to bring the colt under control, something in Jill's mind was saying, "This isn't right. Dawn has never acted like this. *Dawn isn't afraid of strangers.*"

It took Jill a full minute to quiet the colt. Then the judge

went over him carefully. But Dawn's sides were still heaving, and Jill knew with a sinking heart that Dawn had lost.

Jill watched the blue ribbon pinned on the saddle-horse filly. And the red pinned on the Tennessee walking horse. She saw the third place go to the palomino colt.

As Jill led Dawn out of the ring, Jo Ann was the first to throw her arms around her sister. "You were wonderful," she said loyally. "It wasn't your fault that Dawn was scared. The judge should have given you a prize anyway."

Jill's mother said, "We're very proud of you, dear. And proud of Dawn, too. Remember, he's just a baby. Everything was strange to him. Don't blame him for being frightened."

Jill's father said, "It's too bad everyone can't win, Jilly. But you made a good try. Remember, you and Dawn got right up to the final judging. That's a good job for your first year's work with a colt."

Back in the stall, rubbing down her colt, Jill shook her head, trying to shake the tears out of her eyes. "It wasn't your fault, Dawn," she whispered. "I'm just sure it wasn't. You'll be at home with Dolly tonight. And losing isn't half as hard when you have a family to help you."

The last event of the day was the class in horsemanship. This was the event when Alex would ride Laddie.

Again Jill stood on the side lines, and again she felt she could hardly bear the suspense of watching, as Alex rode into the ring. Hoping so desperately that Alex would win, she almost forgot her own disappointment.

Laddie started off smartly. The palomino was in perfect form as he led the other horses around the ring. Alex sat straight and slim in the saddle. His hands on the reins were light. He looked straight ahead and there was no sign in his face of what he might be feeling. At the command to trot, Laddie went into a smooth pace, horse and rider moving so perfectly they seemed meant to travel together. Round and round they went—walk, trot, canter, change leads; reverse. With each new command from the judge, Alex guided his horse expertly.

It was no surprise to the audience when, without hesitation, the judge put the blue ribbon on Laddie's bridle. Laddie's performance, and his rider's, had been easily the best in the field. A wave of applause went through the stands. Jill clapped until her palms smarted, and she beamed with pride for Alex. Now surely Alex will be happy, she thought. If only this will change Alex. If it will make him realize that good things do happen. . . .

"It was a wonderful fair, except that Jill and Dawn didn't win a prize," Jo Ann said on the way home that night. "Scotty said he was proud of all the 4-H clubs. But I'm sure he was really proudest of the Merrymakers. Don't you think so, Jill?"

"M'mm," Jill agreed. She smiled in the darkness at Jo-Jo's tone of innocent assurance.

There was one thing about little sisters, she decided. Sometimes they could make you feel awfully old, and wise.

Everyone agreed that Alex had been a star performer for the Merrymakers. "At least a dozen people have told me how impressed they were with the way the boy rode," Mr. Miller said a few days later. "Scotty says it was the best exhibition of horsemanship he's ever seen a boy give."

"Alex is sure to win the horsemanship class at the State Fair." Mrs. Miller nodded.

"*If* he can go—" Mr. Miller looked worried. "The trouble is that is costs money to take a horse to the fair. Ed Marshall says Alex hasn't enough money of his own to swing the expense. It seems his mother has been sick again, and Alex has been sending her everything he's earned at his job. That's why he wouldn't take time off from work to go to Rock Springs with the others. It's a shame, when he's done such a terrific job with Laddie."

Jill listened with dismay. It made her feel proud to hear Alex praised, but it didn't seem fair that he couldn't take Laddie to Hutchinson when he had earned the right to. Lois Barnes was taking her winning sheep, and Sally was going to show Pete at the State Fair. Even Jo-Jo was in a tizzy over taking her angel-food cake. If only Dawn had won a ribbon, I might be taking him, too, Jill thought, but she caught herself up sharply. She remembered what Chuck had taught her when she was a little girl.

"When something bad happens," Chuck used to tell her, "cry hard and get it over with. But for the love of Pete don't go around whining afterward. That is, if you want anybody to like you."

"All right, I *won't* whine about Dawn," Jill told herself firmly. "But I wish, I just wish that somehow Alex could take Laddie to the fair!"

If I'd wished on a horseshoe and a four-leaf clover and a rabbit's foot and a shooting star all together, the wish couldn't come true any faster, Jill thought later.

That same afternoon Mr. Miller came home with the news that the men at the feed store in Dale Valley, where

Alex worked, wanted to send him to Hutchinson. So he would be able to take Laddie to the State Fair after all.

Jill could scarcely believe her ears when her father told them. But when Alex stopped by the next morning with more good news, she thought she must really be dreaming.

Alex was waving a paper in his hand. It was a letter, addressed to the Merrymakers 4-H Saddle Club, and it said that the Dale County Fair officials had reconsidered the case of Miss Jill Miller.

"Dr. Young was at the fair," Alex explained, before Jill could finish reading the letter. "He talked to two people who were standing right next to the ring when Dawn was being shown. They both told him that a boy had thrown a dart and hit Dawn. That's what made Dawn bolt. When Dr. Young told the Fair Committee what had happened, they said Dawn ought to have another chance. This letter says you can take Dawn to the State Fair."

Jill was ready to let out a whoop of sheer excitement, but Alex stopped her quickly.

"If you're going to show Dawn again," he said, "you'll be up against really stiff competition. You'll have to practice every day."

"I'll practice every minute," Jill said happily. "I'll do anything you tell me if Dawn can have another chance."

For the next hour Alex worked with Jill, showing her again how to lead the colt, how to coax him to stand quietly, how to make the most of his good points for the judge's inspection.

It wasn't until the lesson was over, and Alex had left, that Jill had time to rush into the house and telephone Sally the breathless news that Alex was taking Laddie to the State Fair, and that she and Dawn would be going, too.

CHAPTER 17

Charger

"I just didn't think it could go on being this hot, but it did," Jill said in the early afternoon when they drove into the State Fair grounds. She climbed out of the Pattersons' station wagon and stretched her legs stiffly after the long drive. "I feel as though I've been sitting in one spot forever and that spot was an oven!" Jill mopped her forehead.

"Oh, stop complaining," Sally said. "You've said a thousand times these last six months that if you could just bring Dawn to the fair, you'd be satisfied. So now, here we are! Anyway"—she climbed out after Jill, and squinted up at the sky—"it's clouding over. Let's hope it rains before tonight and cools us off."

"I'm not waiting for rain," Jill said, as the girls carried their luggage into the dormitory room they were to share. Carol and Jo Ann would have a room across the hall. Jill put her bag on one of the beds and kicked off her loafers. "Me for a shower, right now. A nice cold one. Then let's get unpacked and into some clean clothes and over to meet the trucks with the animals. I'm dying to see how Dawn made the trip."

Jill was still splashing in the shower, and Sally was waiting for her turn, when the Millers' car drove up outside. Carol had driven over with Chuck and Jo Ann and Mr. and Mrs. Miller.

Sally hurried out to help them unload suitcases,

"Don't touch anything until I take out my cake," Jo-Jo warned. She reached in and backed out cautiously, balancing the precious angel-food ring, covered with layers of wax paper and foil. "I just hope it's still all right." Jo Ann peeped carefully under the wrappings.

Carol was already out of the car. Her eyes sparkled with excitement as she followed Sally into the dormitory, waving a yellow paper in her hand. "Sally! Jill! I have the most wonderful news!" Carol called. "A telegram came just after you left this morning. It says I've been accepted for training at the Center City Hospital in Michigan! That's the hospital I visited last summer, where I met Kenny when he was a patient in the rheumatic-fever ward."

Carol went on, her eyes still shining, "It's the most wonderful hospital, and I'll be doing just the work I love the most—taking care of children. And Kenny's family have asked me to live with them while I'm training. Of course, I'll be staying at the hospital most of the time; but on weekends and my days off, I'll have a family to go home to. And that's not all. I had a letter from Kenny. He says that 4-H clubs are being started in Center City. He'll have a chance to belong to one, and he's thrilled. Now he can be a real 4-H'er instead of just honorary. He's already made me promise to be a leader in the new club."

"Oh, Carol. It sounds marvelous." Sally beamed.

Jill had come out of the shower just in time to hear the news. She flung herself damply on Carol. "It's wonderful," she said. "Being a nurse is what you've dreamed of all these years. I'm so happy." She gave Carol an enthusiastic squeeze, but the next moment she drew back, her face sober.

Suddenly Jill realized what a change this would make in her life. Ever since she could remember, Jill had looked up to Carol and followed Carol. She had always told Carol her troubles. Beginning when she was just a little girl, she had tried to be exactly like Carol. She had copied Carol's clothes, and begged to let her hair grow so it would look like Carol's. Carol had helped her with her lessons and coaxed her to try out for her first play at school. It was Carol who had persuaded Jill's mother, just that year, that Jill was old enough to use lipstick. All Jill's life, Carol had always been there.

Now, suddenly, Jill realized that Carol would be gone.

"I know it's what you want to do, but if only you didn't have to go away to do it," Jill wailed. "Oh, I don't see why good things can't happen to people without changing everything for other people." Jill's hair was still dripping from the shower. It hung in wet streaks on her round cheeks, making her look almost like a little girl again. But her expression was tragic.

As Carol looked back, the radiant happiness in her own face clouded for a moment. "I wish so, too, Jilly," she said slowly. "I wish I didn't have to leave everything here—my family, and all of you, and school, and the Merrymakers, and all the fun—and Johnny—"

The last word was only a whisper. But looking into Carol's eyes, Jill felt ashamed. The moment before she had been thinking only of her own loneliness. Now she saw how much harder it would be for Carol. It was Carol who would be going away alone, so far from everything she knew—so far from Johnny. Jill couldn't find any words to say what she wanted to. She only patted Carol's shoulder, wanting somehow to comfort the older girl.

The clouds that had been gathering faintly in the sky were darkening. When a sharp gust of wind rattled the windows, the girls went to look out anxiously.

"It's going to pour," Jill said anxiously. "We'll have to hurry to meet the trucks before we get drowned. I don't want Dawn to get wet before I put him into his stall."

"And my cake!" Jo-Jo exclaimed in alarm. "I'm supposed to take it to the exhibit in the Main Hall. If it gets rained on it'll be ruined."

The girls hurried as fast as they could, but the sky had turned almost black, and a few raindrops fell on the dry, dusty ground like bits of heavy lead.

Jo Ann managed to dodge the drops. She delivered her cake safely, and watched it being put up on the exhibit table with a long sigh of relief. Then she ran to join the other girls in one of the 4-H buildings just as the rain came pelting down. She found them with a group which had gathered around a boy who had a portable radio. They were listening to a weather broadcast.

There had been flash floods along the highways, the radio announcer said. Some of the roads near Hutchinson were washed out.

"That means our trucks will be held up," Jill said to Sally. The girls looked at each other anxiously.

A few minutes later they were relieved to see Scotty come toward them. He shook the rain off the shoulders of his jacket. It was true about the flash flood, Scotty said, answering the girls' questions. But he had just had a phone call from the driver of one of the trucks. They'd be delayed another two hours or so, but everything was under control. The rains had stopped, and the animals were all fine.

"There's no use our waiting here," Scotty said. "Let's find the rest of the Merrymakers and go get some supper."

They gathered in a group and made a dash through the rain for the cafeteria. There was a juke box at the end of the dining hall, and a space for dancing. When they had devoured plates of cheeseburgers and potato salad, Tim and Jerry collected quarters, and they each put in requests for their favorite records.

Before long the Merrymakers had forgotten the long day's trip and the rain outside.

Jill even forgot to be anxious about Dawn. She had been surprised and pleased when Alex joined their group for supper. She was even more surprised when he asked her to dance. It was the first time he had ever asked any of the girls. Jill had always supposed it was because Alex didn't know how to dance. To her astonishment, he danced very well—even better than Gig Williamson. It's taken a long enough time, Jill thought, following his steps dreamily, but maybe Alex has finally decided to like us!

They got back to find that the trucks had just rolled in. The beef calves were being unloaded, and Sally rushed to meet Pete.

Next came the truck with the horses. As Jill stood waiting for Dawn, she saw Laddie start down the ramp. Alex went to take Laddie's halter.

The next moment there was a crash and a sound of splintering wood.

Jill looked over to see Laddie floundering. The palomino

had stumbled somehow, coming down the ramp. He struggled to get his footing again, then, with Alex leading him, Laddie limped off toward his stall.

Jill had caught only a glimpse of Alex's white face, but it was enough to frighten her. She would have turned to follow him; but at that moment Dawn was led out of the truck, and Jill hurried to meet her colt.

Dawn stepped down daintily, his little ears pricked sharply as he craned his neck to see what new sights he could find on this latest journey. Jill patted his neck, but her mind was only half on the colt as she settled him in his stall.

What could have happened to Laddie? Why did Alex's face look like that? Jill asked herself.

The moment Jill could leave Dawn, she hurried down the row of stalls. Most of the horses and colts had been bedded for the night and the owners had gone home.

In one of the last stalls, Jim found Alex bending over Laddie's leg. At the sound of Jill's footstep, Alex turned.

"Laddie's lame," Alex said. He spoke very quietly, but there was something in his voice that sent a shiver up Jill's spine. Alex's face was still white. Only his eyes burned.

"Laddie's lame," he repeated. "He hurt himself, coming off the truck. It's his bad leg again."

Jill looked down in dismay. She saw the palomino's swollen, quivering leg. "Oh, Alex"—she began—"how could it have happened?"

"He stumbled," Alex said. "Laddie stumbled coming off the truck, and twisted his leg. I didn't watch where he stepped. *It was my fault.*"

Alex still spoke quietly, yet Jill felt another shiver. Something is the matter with Alex, she thought. It's something much worse than what's happened to Laddie's leg. Maybe it's the thing that has always made him seem so strange— and shut away from people.

A moment later Jill was relieved to see Scotty hurrying toward them. Scotty could always make things right. Surely he would make Alex see that what had happened to Laddie wasn't Alex's fault. He'd make Alex understand that it was an accident—like what had happened to Cuddles at the County Fair.

Jill saw Scotty lean down to examine the palomino's leg. She heard his voice, steady and reassuring, telling Alex that Dr. Young was coming over to the fair tomorrow. Doc would look at Laddie's leg first thing in the morning. Maybe it was nothing bad. Maybe Laddie would be ready for the show tomorrow.

Jill heard Alex answer, quietly again. Yet she had the strange feeling that Alex had not heard a single word that Scotty had said. She followed Alex and Scotty as they went to the door. Then, just as they said good-night, Jill looked down and saw Alex's hands.

They were clenched in the same tight fists she had seen before.

Alex was already walking away. It was almost dusk. Jill had told Sally and the others she would meet them in the dormitory. But just as Alex swung around a corner and disappeared, Jill knew suddenly that she couldn't let him go alone. She turned and ran after him. There was no use calling—she knew he wouldn't turn back—she could only follow, saving her breath to keep up with his long strides, as he hurried toward the gates and out along the side path that led away from the road through a vacant lot. At the end of the path Alex finally stopped.

Jill drew a long breath for courage. Now that she had come this far, what could she say that would make Alex listen? Suppose he were angry because she had followed him? It didn't matter. Even if he wouldn't listen, even if he were furious with her, Jill knew she had been right to come. At least Alex would know that someone was there.

Jill took a step forward and felt her knees shake. "Hi, Alex," she said.

He turned. "Oh—hi," he said. There was no expression in his voice.

At least he didn't sound angry, Jill thought in relief. She took another breath. "I—I—saw you starting out this way, so I thought I'd come along." She struggled to find the right words. "I wanted to tell you how terribly sorry I am about Laddie's leg. I guess it's like Scotty says, these things happen. It's just bad luck."

"Oh, sure. They happen." Alex spoke in the same strangely quiet voice. "It's just my bad luck. *My rotten luck.*" He whipped out the words with sudden anger.

Jill tried to swallow, but her throat felt dry as dust. For a moment she could only stare back at the bitterness that blazed in the boy's eyes. Even if she could find words, Alex wouldn't hear them. Even if she could think of some way to tell him the thing she knew in her heart—that there was no such thing as a fate that made one person's luck better or worse than others, that he only imagined things were always against him—it would have been no use.

Before Jill could speak, Alex went on. "I remember when Charger hurt his leg. That was bad luck, too—" Alex paused.

This time Jill didn't try to answer. Not since the day long ago at the ranch had she heard Alex mention Charger's name. She remembered how odd he had seemed about it

then. Now she was afraid to speak. If she said the wrong thing he might stop suddenly, the way he had before.

This time, instead of stopping, Alex went on. Suddenly he was telling her about Charger as a colt. About breaking him to the saddle, and training him to jump. "The other horses would refuse the jumps at first," Alex said. "But not Charger. He sailed over like a bird."

Alex even smiled as he told about some of Charger's tricks. How he would nose into people's pockets to find carrots. How he would reach over with his nose and nudge Alex's cap over his eyes just when he was trying to tighten a girth.

"He sounds like Dolly." Jill laughed. "The way she puts her head in the air so I can't reach her to put a bridle on."

Jill paused. Somewhere in the back of her mind she

remembered Carol and Sally and Jo-Jo. It was past the time when she had promised to meet them at the dormitory. They'd wonder what had happened. But she brushed the thought away. They'd just have to wait. She could explain later. Right now the important thing was that Alex wanted to talk. For the first time since any of them had known him, Alex seemed to want to tell something about the past that had troubled him. He had kept it shut up inside of him so long—now if he wanted to speak, Jill realized that someone must be there to listen.

"It must have been wonderful having a horse like Charger," Jill said, choosing her words cautiously. "I mean, having him always belong to you."

There was a silence. When Alex finally spoke, his voice had lost all the life it had a few moments before. "*Charger never belonged to me*," he said flatly.

There was another pause. Jill felt her heart sink. Somehow she had said the wrong thing again. Now Alex wouldn't tell her any more. In the deepening dusk she saw him half turn away.

Then suddenly he turned back and went on speaking, not easily, as he had before, but in an angry rush of words. "Charger never belonged to me," he said again. "I was there when he was born. I took care of him. I was the one who took him out to pasture the first time, and saddled him the first time, and taught him how to jump. But Charger was never mine—*not even the night they killed him*."

The last words were flung out like a whip. Jill felt as though they had struck her in the face.

"Killed—" she echoed in horror. "Oh, not Charger killed. . . ."

The strange story came bursting out then. It seemed that

Alex could hardly speak the words fast enough to get them said.

Jill listened, frozen, scarcely able to believe what she heard.

Charger had belonged to a man who lived near his family's home, Alex began. Alex was hardly more than a little boy, but he had loved horses even then. He had been around the barn from the earliest days he could remember, making friends with all the horses. But on the morning that Charger was born, something special seemed to happen. The new colt was like his own.

From that day the boy had spent every hour he could with Charger—feeding and grooming him, breaking him to halter, schooling him in riding manners. Charger knew no other master except Alex.

The owner of the colt hadn't minded. "He was away a lot, traveling," Alex said. "And when he was at home, he was always busy. There was only one groom to take care of the stable—an old man who had been there for years. He was glad enough to let someone else train the colt."

The story went on—how Charger had developed into a beautiful jumper, how Alex had schooled him carefully and patiently. The boy had studied every book he could find about horses. He went to other stables where he could watch the trainers work their horses. "I used to listen to them talk," Alex said. "Sometimes I'd even find a veterinarian who would answer my questions and I'd ask him everything I wanted to know about horses. Then I'd go back and try to teach Charger all I had learned from the trainers. It wasn't hard. Charger was born with good manners and he was a natural jumper. Everyone who saw him jump said he'd be a big winner someday."

Alex told how the man who owned Charger had promised one day he'd give Alex a chance to ride the horse in a show that was coming in the spring. After that Alex had worked even harder training his horse to perfection. He was sure Charger would win—until one day, a week before the show.

Alex had let Charger out to pasture in the afternoon, intending to come back and bring him in before dark. Alex hadn't noticed a place where the pasture fence was broken and some rusty nails stuck out. Somehow Charger had run against the fence and the nails had torn his leg. By the time Alex went back to find him, Charger was gashed and bleeding. They called the veterinarian, but in spite of anything that could be done, the leg was badly infected.

"I knew Charger would never jump again," Alex said. "I knew it was my fault. No one blamed me, but *I knew it.*" His voice was hard.

Days had gone by, and weeks; still Charger's leg was no better. The doctor had finally told Charger's owner that there was no hope that the horse would ever jump again. Even if the leg healed, the horse would always limp.

"The man who owned Charger didn't want a horse that limped. He didn't want any horse that wasn't perfect," Alex spoke bitterly. "So he gave the order for Charger to be shot."

"Oh, no—" Jill breathed the words. She covered her face with her hands. She looked up as Alex's story went on.

"When I heard about the order," he said, "I forgot how afraid I'd always been of Charger's owner. I forgot everything except that I had to save Charger. I went to the big house that day. I talked to the man; I told him I was sure that care and exercise would make Charger's leg heal. *I knew I could make Charger well,* and I begged for the chance. I begged until the man finally promised—" Alex paused. Then he added in the hard, cold voice, "He promised—just to get rid of me."

Jill felt a sick fear go through her. She could hardly bear to listen as Alex finished the story.

"I suppose I believed him," Alex said. "I went home for supper. I even went to sleep that night. But I woke up early and I went straight to the barn. It was hardly daylight when I looked into Charger's stall. It was empty. Charger was dead. They had shot him."

"Oh, Alex—" Jill put her hands over her eyes again.

"I suppose," Alex went on quite calmly, "they meant to do it so that I wouldn't know what had happened. The groom said that they meant to tell me that Charger had died in the night. I remember walking home. I remember wishing they had shot me, too."

When Alex stopped speaking, Jill was crying. Her head was bent to hide the tears, but she didn't need to see Alex's hands to know that they were clenched into fists. She didn't need to wonder any longer why Alex didn't trust people, why he was so sure people never could be really good. She didn't need to wonder any longer why Alex would never trust himself.

Each time before when Jill had seen Alex's hands clenched like that, she had been helpless. She had found no way to speak to him.

This time it was different.

Jill's own hands tightened into fists. Her knuckles were as white as Alex's. She flung her head up. "Alex Marshall, you listen to me." Tears choked her words, but she wasn't afraid to speak now. "You listen to me, Alex. It was a terrible thing

136

that happened to Charger. But you're wrong to go on think-ing you can't ever trust anyone again. You told me I was dumb once. And I was dumb," she went on, astonished to hear her own words. "But I tried to stop being dumb. I tried my level best."

Jill squeezed her fists tighter. Alex didn't speak. No ex-pression flickered across his face.

"It wasn't your fault that Charger hurt himself," Jill plunged desperately on. "I know how dreadful it was to have Charger killed; but if you won't ever trust anyone again —if you won't trust Johnny, or Carol, or Scotty, or me, or yourself—then *you're* being dumb!"

Jill drew one last, long, quivering breath and waited.

"Sure, maybe I've been dumb." As Alex spoke, Jill opened her fists slowly. "But maybe you don't understand," Alex went on, stubbornly. "I've been mad a long time. Ever since Charger was shot. Then I found Laddie. I've worked hard with him. Now it's my fault that he's hurt. But I wanted him to win tomorrow—"

"I know, but so did *we*." Jill flung the words back. She was just as angry as Alex now. Whether he wanted to or not, she would make Alex listen. "Just remember, we all wanted Laddie to win. Scotty and Carol and Chuck and Johnny and Jo-Jo—every single one of us wanted Laddie to win just as much as you did. I don't care whether you trust us or not, but *we're your friends*."

For a minute, a very long minute, the two looked straight at each other.

Then Jill said, "We'd better be getting back. The others will be waiting for me."

They were silent, walking together. When they came to

the dormitory steps, Alex said good-night politely. Then he turned and walked away.

Jill was thankful that the other girls were already in bed when she came in. It hadn't been any use, trying to help Alex, she thought. She undressed, and crept into bed.

It hadn't been any use at all.

She closed her eyes wearily.

CHAPTER 18

Blue Ribbon

Jill awoke the next morning feeling as though she had come up through a deep, troubled sea—through miles of sleep, and the sound of voices that were half dreams and half real. Finally she was awake. Sally was shaking her.

"For heaven's sake, can't you hear me?" Sally shouted. "Are you deaf?"

"No, but I will be if you don't stop yelling in my ear." Jill buried her head deeper in the pillow. Then suddenly she remembered, this was the day of the fair.

She sat up straight, shaking the last sleep out of her eyes. *This was the day Dawn might win a ribbon.* But she had hardly put one foot out of bed before other memories came crowding back—of Laddie's accident the evening before; of the terrible story Alex had told her; of the way she had fought back, trying to break down the wall he had built up against people. She remembered how bitterly disappointed she had been when he still wouldn't listen.

Brushing her teeth, Jill frowned, wondering how Alex would be today. If Dr. Young said Laddie couldn't be shown, would Alex go on feeling that luck always had to be against him?

During breakfast, while Sally rattled on about who

would be judging the Hereford class and how she'd absolutely die if Pete slipped his show halter, Jill only half listened. She sipped her milk and nibbled at her scrambled eggs, but all the while her mind was racing toward the day ahead.

Jill went straight to Dawn's stall. She knew Sally would spend the morning scrubbing and grooming Pete for the judging. Jill found Dawn ready to greet her. But even as she stroked the velvety nose, Jill was looking toward Laddie's stall and wondering what had happened.

A little later, after she had taken care of Dawn, Jill went to look. Laddie was alone in his stall. There was no sign of Alex. Suppose, Jill thought, Alex has gone off somewhere? Suppose he's even more upset after talking about Charger? Suppose Alex had even done something desperate. . . .

Jill came out of the building. The fairgrounds were crowded now. People were everywhere, moving and talking, crowding the walks. It was hopeless to try to guess which way Alex might have gone. Still, she felt she must find him. She found herself hurrying faster and faster through buildings, around corners, watching each face as she passed.

Suddenly Jill stopped at the sight of a familiar figure. It was Dr. Young. Jill hurried to ask him if he had seen Alex.

Dr. Young nodded. "About half an hour ago," he said, "Alex and I looked over Laddie together. It's too bad the horse can't possibly be shown. I bandaged his leg. Luckily there's no real damage. Laddie ought to mend as good as new in a few weeks. But it was hard luck for Alex."

"Thank you," Jill said, and turned away. She felt worse than ever. "*Hard luck for Alex*," Dr. Young had said. But Dr. Young didn't understand what it meant to Alex. No one could understand who hadn't heard the story Jill had heard the night before.

Jill remembered Alex's bitter words again as she pushed on through the crowd. She had to find him somehow. She had to try, one more time, to tell him he wasn't alone. To make him understand.

She retraced her steps, back through the buildings, past line after line of booths. Here and there she caught sight of other Merrymakers. She saw Sally leading Pete away from the washing rack. She bumped into Lois leading her two Hampshire lambs into their pen. They had been blocked and carded until they looked like square white snowballs.

"Don't cough. Don't sneeze. Please don't breathe," Lois begged. "I don't want one speck of dust to get on Ara and Bella." She penned the sheep in, buckled white sheets over them to keep them clean, and collapsed with a sigh. "Now I can relax," she said. She fanned herself with a wide-brimmed straw hat, being careful to fan Ara and Bella at the same time. "What's the news?" she asked Jill. "Have the Merrymakers won any ribbons?"

Jill nodded. "We got Honorable Mention for our booth. Tim has a red ribbon for his wheat, and Billie Jeanne's tomatoes got a blue. That's about all I know so far." Jill's glance wandered as she spoke, searching the crowd of passers-by. She waved good-by to Lois and went on, still searching for Alex.

The sun grew hotter. Jill was tired and thirsty. Her eyes ached from looking at hundreds of strange faces. She would have loved to stop for a cold drink, but she didn't dare. She might miss seeing Alex.

She hadn't realized how long she had walked until she

saw Jerry Patterson coming through the crowd, waving at her. "Hey, Jill, it's almost time to take the colts in to show," Jerry called. "Where on earth have you been? You'd better hurry if you're going to have Dawn ready."

Dawn! Jill had almost forgotten him. She looked at her watch, horrified. There was barely half an hour left before Dawn must be in the ring, and she still had to give him his last grooming.

She raced back to the stall and stopped in astonishment. Dawn stood waiting, groomed and ready to show. His coat had been curried until it was smooth as velvet. His halter was on. His hoofs were polished and shining. Jill stared in wonder. No one could have made Dawn look so perfect except Alex, Jill thought.

Alex must have been here. "While I was hunting for him all over the fairgrounds, he must have been right here," Jill told herself. She looked around, with one last hope of finding him, but there was no one in sight. Most of the stalls were empty. The owners had already taken their horses to the ring.

There was no time to search any longer. Jill stopped only long enough to smooth her hair and tuck in her blouse, hoping she looked neat enough for the show ring, before she led Dawn out.

Jill joined the others at the edge of the ring. Waiting to be called before the judges, no one spoke much. The colts frisked like puppies, rolling their eyes at each other, kicking playfully, and nipping with their sharp little teeth. Their owners tried to quiet them.

A girl standing next to Jill pulled her colt's head up sharply. "Honestly," she sighed, "aren't they awful? I thought I had Bluebell trained so nicely at home. But when she sees the other colts she just acts crazy!"

Jill nodded. She tugged on Dawn's halter just in time to keep him from putting his inquisitive little nose into a passer-by's ice-cream cone. She stroked the colt's neck and felt him quiver with excitement under her hand. Her own throat was dry with nervousness.

When Jill heard her number called, she stepped out before the judges. Until this very last moment she had still hoped to find Alex. Now it was too late. There was nothing to do but try to remember everything Alex had told her about handling Dawn.

"Keep his head high. Make him step carefully. Watch his gait." Jill could almost hear Alex's voice saying the words as she took Dawn around the ring, first at a walk, then at a trot, and brought him to a halt and stretch, holding him steady while the judge walked back and forth studying each colt from every angle. This time Dawn held the stretch perfectly. Alex would have been pleased, Jill thought, as she felt her own knees beginning to shake. She seemed to hear Alex's words again. *"Remember, all horses are mind readers. The minute you're nervous, your horse knows it. Then he'll be nervous, too."* Jill tried desperately to feel calm.

One by one the colts were eliminated until only four were left for the final judging. Dawn was still in the ring. When Jill led Dawn the last time around before the judge, she whispered, "Remember, Dawn—be *proud*." The colt lifted his head as though he really understood. He picked his feet up daintily, and set them down smartly. He arched his neck for everyone to see. As they finished the round and Jill brought Dawn back to a halt, she heard, as if it came from a million miles away, the spatter of applause. "Good boy," she said under her breath. "Good Dawn." In that one minute Jill felt paid back for every hour of care she had spent on him.

There was the last, endless wait. The judge had the ribbons in his hand now. He was looking at his notes. He paused and looked slowly from Dawn to a saddle-horse colt.

For one horrible minute Jill thought she was going to faint. Then she remembered hearing her mother say, "No one has fainted in our family for three generations." She certainly wasn't going to be the first one! She remembered her first-aid training, and took long, deep breaths.

The judge was walking toward her.

Jill forgot all about first-aid and held her breath.

The judge pinned the blue ribbon on Dawn's halter. He patted Dawn's neck, and smiled at Jill. She could hear the crowd clapping loudly now. Jill closed her eyes. In that moment she seemed to remember a hundred things—the day she had begged her father and Alex to let her take care of Dolly, the mornings she had staggered out of bed and gone down to the cold barn to take care of the little mare, the moment she had looked down at Dawn's funny-looking new-born face, the months she had spent training him. And now the blue ribbon, pinned on Dawn's halter.

Jill looked up. But before she could thank the judge, she saw something that drove every other thought out of her mind.

Alex was standing just outside the ring.

Alex had his hands up, clapping as hard as he could. And the smile on his face was as wide as a sunrise.

It was almost more than Jill could believe. Alex was clapping because she and Dawn had won. Alex was smiling as though his whole heart were in it. *Alex looked happy!*

The next minute there were people all around. A photographer was taking a picture of Jill and Dawn for the newspapers. A reporter was asking Jill's name and where she lived. When Jill finally led Dawn back to the stall, Sally was hugging her from one side, her mother was kissing her cheek from the other side. Her father was reaching across to pound her shoulder. "Good girl, Jilly." She could hear Daddy's voice above the others. Lois and Jerry were shouting at her. Scotty came up to shake her hand.

Jill was laughing. "My heavens, I feel as though I've won the Kentucky Derby or something."

She had taken Dawn back to the stall before Jill realized that she hadn't seen Alex since he had stood outside the ring. But this time Jill didn't worry. She remembered Alex clapping, Alex smiling, and somehow she knew Alex was all right now.

When Sally pushed a hot dog with sauerkraut into Jill's hand, Jill realized something else. She hadn't eaten a thing since breakfast, and that seemed like at least a year ago.

"No wonder I almost fainted in front of the judge and disgraced the family!" Jill said through a mouthful. "I was starving!"

She had hardly swallowed the last bite before a small figure hurled itself at her like a cannon ball. It was Jo Ann. She burst into the stall and flung her arms around Jill.

"Jill, I just heard about Dawn winning," Jo-Jo gasped breathlessly. "It's just wonderful. I knew he would. And oh, guess what else, Jill? My angel-food cake just got a second-prize ribbon! Do you know what that means?" Jo Ann looked up earnestly. Her face was streaked with dust and there was a ring of chocolate ice cream around her mouth. But her eyes were shining. "It means I baked one of the second-best cakes in the state of Kansas, that's what it means," Jo Ann finished solemnly.

"Jo-Jo, that's marvelous." Jill hugged her younger sister. "If one more good thing happens today," she said, laughing, "I can't stand it. I'll die of happiness!"

Two more things happened.

Sally's calf, Pete, was sold for a fancy price. Sally came dashing back with the check in her hand. "I'm putting the money in the bank tomorrow," she said. "With what I earned from Fat Stuff and Hot Stuff last year, and this, Daddy says I have enough to start me off at college. Then I can really be a teacher."

The last good thing was when Johnny Lane drove over for the last day of the fair with the news that his brother Bill had a discharge from the Army. Bill would be home by the first of the year. Then he would take over the Lane ranch. Johnny would be free to start studying at medical school.

"I never knew such a happy day," Jill said, when she fell asleep that night.

CHAPTER 19

Lucky Clover

Jill put the last T-shirt and a pair of socks into her suitcase the next morning and sat down on the bed. She leaned her head against the wall and closed her eyes. "I've never been so tired in all my life," she said. "I'm going to go to sleep the minute we get in the car and not wake up until we're home. But, oh my"—she drew a long, deep breath—"hasn't it been fun?"

When no one answered, Jill opened her eyes. Sally was sitting on the bed opposite, her face serious. Jo Ann was cross-legged on the floor; she held her precious ribbon on one knee. Carol stood at the window, looking out. The cloud of her light hair fell around her shoulders, as golden as the sunshine outside. But her expression was sober.

There was silence for a long moment. Each of them was lost in her own thoughts.

Finally Jo Ann said softly, "I just never thought I'd win anything at a State Fair." She stroked her ribbon lovingly. "I just never thought I would."

"A week from tonight I'll be on my way to Michigan," Carol said.

"And I'll be back in school," Sally said. "I'll really have

to study if I'm going to get good enough marks to go to college."

Jill said nothing. She was thinking of how many things had changed in the last year. And how many changes were still to come. She wasn't sure yet what she wanted most—not really sure the way Carol or Johnny or Sally were. Or even Jo-Jo. Jill watched her little sister with a smile. Jo-Jo had won her ribbon. She was sure this was the happiest day she would ever have in her whole life.

A year ago, Jill thought, I would have been sure that winning a ribbon at the State Fair would be *my* happiest day. Now, looking at Jo-Jo holding her ribbon and looking so perfectly happy made Jill feel almost like crying, although she couldn't imagine why.

My heavens, Jill thought in sudden panic, if this is what being grown up is like—if everything is going to be all higgledy-piggledy—then I don't want it! Anyway, not yet.

There was a rap at the door. Jill jumped up to answer. It was a relief to stop thinking such serious thoughts. Johnny and Chuck were outside. Alex was with them.

"All right, gals, we're loading," Chuck said. "Are you all packed?"

The girls picked up suitcases and duffel bags to load in the two cars.

"Alex is driving back with us," Johnny said.

Jill noticed how different Alex seemed. The tense look that had been around his mouth for so long was gone and there was a new confidence in his manner. She saw Alex laugh—really laugh—when Chuck said something funny. It might take time before Alex learned what having friends meant; but if he had started to learn, that was enough, Jill thought happily.

When they had everything stowed away, there was still a wait for Mr. Patterson. They went to sit down in garden chairs on the shady lawn. It was Chuck who leaned down and picked up a four-leaf clover. He held it up for the girls to see.

"Here's a lucky 4-H clover for one of you," he said, looking at the girls. "Which one will it be? I know—" He pulled the leaves carefully apart and handed one to each of the four girls. "There's luck for all four of you," he said. "Just make your wishes."

Carol and Jill and Sally and Jo Ann looked down at the green leaf each one held. Jill could guess what Carol's wish would be, and Sally's. Jo-Jo might be wishing for a blue ribbon at the next fair. Jill hesitated a minute. Then she thought, *I wish next year would be just as nice as this last one.*

Not one of them knew what the year ahead would bring. Johnny and Carol would be far away. Alex might be going even farther to join his family in Alaska. If there were another "H" to add to the first four "H's," it should be for Hope, Jill thought, as she tucked the tiny green leaf carefully into the pocket of her shirt.

It had been a wonderful fair. It was a wonderful life and a wonderful world. But when Jill climbed into the car a few minutes later, she snuggled her head onto a duffel bag with a long sigh.

Right now all she wanted to do was sleep.